SILESIAN FOLK TALES

The book of Rübezahl

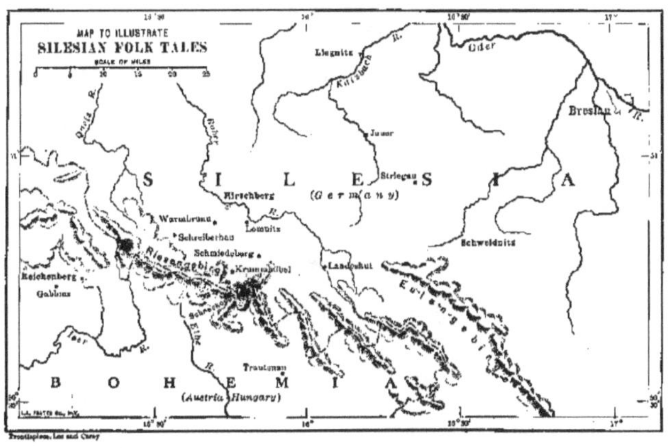

by James Lee, MD and James T. Carey, AM
~*~
(Mildly) Adapted by K. J. Joyner

Silesian Folk Tales: The Book of Rübezahl
Lee,James; Carey, James T.; Joyner, K. J.

With the original illustrations from the 1915 edition

New, adapted edition
2016

Published by The Writers of the Apocalypse
117 N Carbon Street, PMB 208
Marion, IL 62959
www.apocalypsewriters.com

Ebook ISBN: 978-1-944322-16-8
ISBN Print: 978-1-944322-17-5

SILESIAN FOLK TALES
(THE BOOK OF RÜBEZAHL)

James Lee, M.D.
and
James T. Carey, A.M.

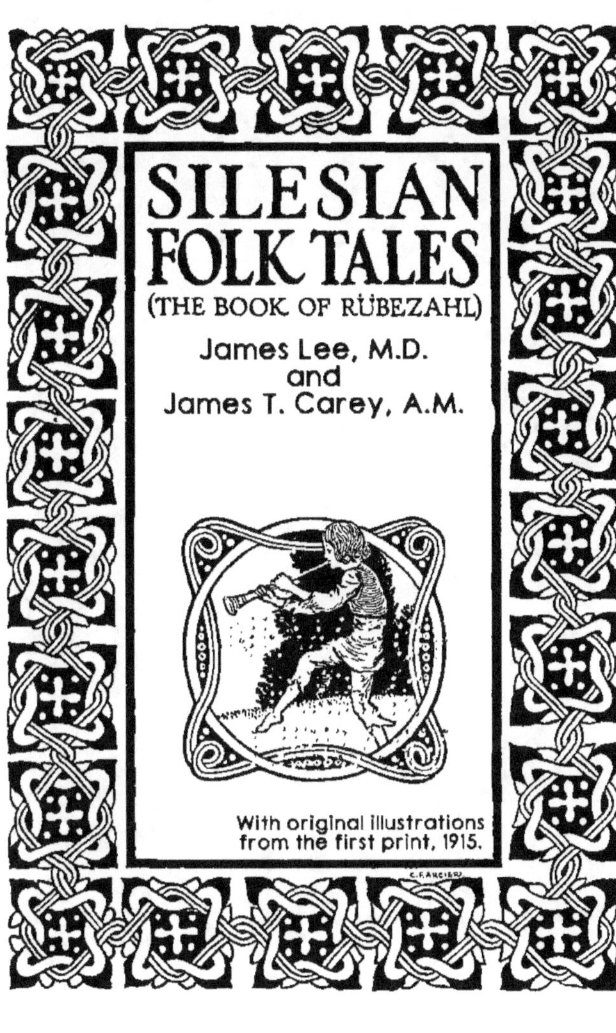

With original illustrations
from the first print, 1915.

(Original) Introduction

The following tales, for the most part, have their scenes laid in Silesia and Bohemia. They are well known throughout all Germany, especially in the central and southern parts. They are folk tales in the highest acceptation of the term. For centuries they have come down in the shape of tradition from generation to generation.

Silesia, the land of their birth, has had an eventful history. Originally a part of Poland, it was drawn under the influence of the German king, Frederick Barbarossa, about 1163. Many names of places suggest that the original population was Celtic. For four centuries it was almost continuously under the domination of Bohemia. It was annexed to that country about 1472. It was finally added to Prussia by Frederick the Great. Bohemia derives its name from a Celtic tribe. It forms the border line between the German and Slavonic races. The geography and history of these countries are very interesting and will repay any reading and study that may be given to them.

Rübezahl, the hero of these tales, to use the words of a now forgotten writer[1] of his adventures, "is a spirit prince and exercises supreme authority over all other gnomes in his district. He is superior to them in many particulars. What his real appearance is no one really knows. He can make himself so beautiful that Apollo is ugly in comparison.

On the other hand, he may, and he often does, assume an appearance so terrible that old women hurriedly mutter a fervent prayer, brave men take to flight, and young maidens sink in unconsciousness. His character is as changeable as his form."

His better side is presented in this little volume, but many stories are told of the manner in which he

---

[1] Lyser

took revenge on mankind for the great injury it inflicted on him and which eventually gave him his popular name.

"Imagine yourselves, my dear readers, seated on a wild winter night in a Silesian hut in the Riesengebirge[2], several thousand feet higher than the surrounding valleys, with snow, fathoms deep, everywhere. The wild storm rages through the desolate mountains. Within, however, everything is warm and comfortable, and as the matrons and maidens busily spin, in fancy, you can listen with pleasure to their tales of the mighty Mountain Lord."

These tales have been carefully adapted for the young readers of the elementary schools, and it is to be hoped that these will derive as much pleasure from their perusal as do their young friends in the different countries of Central Europe.

There, Rübezahl is known as the hero of many a merry prank, and though his character is not entirely free from the charge of spiteful actions, he is, on the whole, a personage with whome it is well that our young folk should become acquainted.

Much has been written about him, though not in English.

In fact, with an exception or two, this is the first collection of Rübezahl to be placed before the American reading public.

The general tone is quietly ethical, and the youngest reader should easily perceive the valuable lessons to be derived from them.

James Lee, MD, and
James T Carey, AM

---

[2] Giant mountains, lofty and rugged, about 23 miles long and 14 miles broad, between Bohemia and Prussian Silesia. They are, next to the Alps, the highest of Central Europe. Schneekoppe is the highest point, being 5264 feet high.

(Modern) Introduction

I'm putting this book back on shelves for the general public in an overall effort to keep it from being lost. Sure it comes from the public domain and there is at least one archive that houses it, but that doesn't mean what we've preserved won't somehow be lost someday.

I have also very sparsely updated or tightened some of the language. I suppose you could call this adapting the book, but I prefer to call it "mildly adapting". Of course I did it to make the book easier to understand for the modern reader, but I had to be careful lest I actually change the stories themselves. This book remains an antiquated read in many respects as a result.

A modern day reader should take note that these stories are from a different generation. At least one story raised my eyebrow at what my modern mind perceived an injustice.

In my youth these sorts of stories, with this very archaic language, would have been delegated to children. A lot of people wouldn't do that today, but maybe they should. Okay yes, the drawback to me reading so many old things is I once got bad marks on a college paper for trying to "fake it" using "Middle English" when the truth is I really do speak this way. But this drawback means something very important: not all of my education depended on being at a desk, bored to death. I learned a lot of things on my own. And I had fun doing it.

So if nothing else, read this to your children. Act out the parts. Have fun with it. That's what these stories were originally for, you know.

K. J. Joyner

TABLE OF CONTENTS

RÜBEZAHL IN THE BEGINNING

NORTH OF THE CZECH REPUBLIC and the South-west of Poland, as part of the Sudetes mountain system, there extends a lofty range of mountains known as the Riesengebirge. Long ago, this area was between two countries, Silesia and Bohemia. Times change and the land often will change with it. Which is how and why Rübezahl begins his tales with us, mere humans.

The name, Giant's Mountains, recalls many legends concerning Rübezahl, who for centuries, according to these legends, held sway there and made the neighborhood the theater of his many wonderful and frightening exploits.

On the earth's surface this prince of the mountain spirits possesses limited territory, a few miles principally on the rocky heights and surrounding country. Beneath the earth's crust his real dominion begins, and it stretches downward to the center of the globe. At times it pleases this ruler of the underworld to wander through his realm, to inspect the treasure chambers of gold and silver, to oversee his subject spirits and other ghostly creatures, and to keep them at work.

During these times when Rübezahl throws off all cares of state, he comes to the earth's surface and lives for a while on the Riesengebirge. In playful wantonness he makes fun and mockery with the children of men. Friend Rübezahl, be it known, is peculiarly composed, peevish, impulsive, violent, malicious, fickle, though at times generous and sympathetic. Like an egg in boiling water he is soft and hard at two successive moments; one day, the warmest friend, the next day, strange and cold; in short, full of contradictions, and acting, generally, according to the impulse of the moment.

Many, many centuries ago, and long before either Silesia or Bohemia (or the Czech Republic for that matter) was inhabited, Rübezahl wandered around the wild mountains. He took pleasure in inciting bears and wild ox[3] to deadly combat, or in driving them over steep cliffs into the valleys below. When he grew tired of hunting, he would return to the underworld and remain there until again the desire would overmaster him to enjoy the beaming sun and the beauties of the surface.

One can imagine how astounded he was on one of these occasions when, looking down from the summit of the Riesengebirge, he found the landscape changed. The once gloomy, impenetrable woods had disappeared and in their place were fruitful fields where rich harvests were ripening. Between budding fruit trees appeared the thatched roofs of comfortable cottages out of whose chimneys blue smoke curled upward. Here and there on the summit of a hill was a solitary watch tower so the people could keep a lookout for danger. Sheep and cattle grazed on the verdant meadows and the sweet tones of the shepherd's flute could be heard in the distance.

The changes delighted him and he was not displeased with the farmers, although they'd settled there without his permission. He decided to leave them in undisturbed possession of the property, as a good-natured farmer allows the twittering swallow or

---

[3] Aurochses, as per the original text, a North European breed.

troublesome sparrow to build in the projecting eaves of his barn. He even wanted to become acquainted with men, and to get used to talking with them.

Rübezahl has the magical gift of being able to change shape. He can change into anything he wants, although when it comes to man he usually assumes the shape of a fellow human. So he took the form of a peasant and found a job with the nearest farmer. Everything he did prospered, and Rips, as he called himself, was soon recognized as the best workman around. But his employer was a spendthrift. He was always spending money and squandered the profits of his faithful laborer, giving Rips but little thanks for his hard work. On this account Rips left him.

His next job was with a shepherd. Rips carefully watched over the flocks of sheep and conducted them to the hillside pastures where rich juicy grass was found in abundance. The flocks thrived, even flourished, under his care. No sheep fell from the overhanging cliffs nor were any eaten by wolves. His master, however, was a greedy miser who poorly repaid his faithful helper. He sometimes even stole the best ewe from his own flock and deducted the price from Rips's wages.

Later on Rips took service with the judge of the village. He became a terror to criminals, and he was very enthusiastic enforcing the law. But the judge was corrupt and decided cases according to his interests and secretly even mocked at the law. When Rips refused to be a tool of injustice he was thrown into prison, from which he escaped in the usual way to spirits, through the keyhole.

These first attempts to get to know mankind in no way increased his love for them, as I'm sure you can imagine. Annoyed, he returned to the summit of the Riesengebirge, looked down over the smiling fields, and wondered how mother nature could shower so many gifts on such thankless creatures.

There was a petty king in the country of Silesia, and he reigned in the area bordering on the Riesengebirge. He had a beautiful daughter named Emma, as kings usually do. The Mountain Lord once saw her as she and her servant maidens were taking a walk.

Immediately he fell in love with her. He went to her father's court and asked for her hand in marriage. He represented himself as a powerful prince from the Far East, just then on his travels. Using his magic, he put on a lavish display of wealth and glory to color to his statement.

Emma's father the king was not against the match, but Emma, who was already engaged to Ratibor, the son of a neighboring prince, positively refused.

Not to be discouraged, the Mountain Lord used his magic and created a palace on the mountains just for the Princess Emma. Then he used his magic to steal Emma away, transporting her to it. Here she was to live as his prisoner until she agreed to marry him.

To keep her from getting lonely, he gave her a magical wand. With it she could change turnips into anything she wanted them to be. She changed a basketful of turnips into people to talk to or pets to care for. She lived pleasantly like this for a long time, surrounded by her counterfeit companions. But she never stopped looking for a way to escape.

After a while she hit on the following plan. The Mountain Lord had planted a large field of turnips so that she should always have a plentiful supply. One day Emma asked him to count the number of plants that had sprouted. She told him she had finally decided to become his wife and needed to know how many people would be coming to her wedding. She said she was going to give life to every turnip in the field. However, she also warned him to be accurate in his count because even a single mistake would change her mind.

Beside himself with joy Rübezahl began his allotted work. He skipped around among the growing turnips as nimbly as a sparrow picking up grains of wheat. Owing to his zeal, he was soon finished but to make sure he had done it right he counted again.

He found to his annoyance that the two counts didn't agree. This meant he had to count a third time. After the third count, there was still a difference in totals. He had been so excited to marry Emma and so preoccupied thinking about it, he had missed his count each time. This meant he had to count the turnips again!

While the simple-hearted Mountain Lord was counting and recounting the turnips, Emma made her escape. Using the wand, she changed a turnip into a magnificent steed. Riding it, she fled over hill and dale until she reached her father's land.

Since that time the people of Silesia in mockery called the Mountain Lord Rübenzahler, turnip counter, or Rübezahl for short. To call him by this name is always sure to rouse him to anger, as we shall learn in the course of our stories.

THE WAGONER

ONE DAY, LONG AGO, Rübezahl was traveling by foot on the highway to Hirschberg.

A wagoner, that is to say someone driving a horse-drawn wagon, was passing by. The wagoner only a light load in his wagon, so journeyman Rübezahl asked for a ride. In return for the favor he offered to pay what little money he had.

The surly wagoner angrily snapped his whip and said gruffly, "I'm not overanxious for a traveling companion, neither are my horses. They have enough to do dragging an empty wagon over these wretched roads. Still, give me the money before you get in. I'll take you, although I don't really trust strangers."

The lad drew out his purse and gave him four groschen, which was the coin back then. Then the journeyman answered laughingly, "Your words should offend me, but I'm willing to swallow the bitter pills; they won't give me a stomachache." He got into the wagon and sat on the hay which lay in the bottom. The wagon moved slowly forward along the deep and uneven ruts.

They'd gone only a short distance when the horses suddenly stood still. The wagoner shouted at them, he cracked his whip, and he even beat them. The horses wouldn't move from the spot. The wagoner angrily looked to see what was wrong with the wagon or harness. He found everything in good condition and was unable to understand the obstinacy of the horses.

"I see," said the journeyman, as he got out of the wagon, "that I can go faster on foot than I can with you and your horses. Give me my money back. I can get supper and lodging for it at Hirschberg, and my feet can carry me that far."

"What is wrong with you, you fool?" the wagoner said mockingly. "What's paid is paid. I didn't force you to get into my wagon and I don't force you to get out. You do so of your own free will. You may keep your seat if it suits you. The balky horses will soon go on again."

But the animals stood stock still, as if made of stone. They didn't even move their ears. Flies gathered around them to bite them, and the horses didn't even switch their tails to shoo them off. The wagoner took a large club and beat the horses in blind rage. After stopping for breath, he was about to renew his attack when both animals fell suddenly to the ground as if dead.

"A wicked spell rests on the horses," he murmured, and looked suspiciously at the journeyman, who was now sitting by the roadside to eat his frugal lunch. "Don't you also think that the horses are bewitched?"

"How do I know?" was the answer. "Let me help you." The journeyman got up and slung his wallet over his shoulders. He went to one of the horses, unhitched it, and patted it coaxingly on the neck.

The horse suddenly sprang to its feet and the lad leaped upon its back. They galloped away at great speed. As a farewell he waved his hat to the astonished wagoner and cried out laughingly, "I thank you for the seat in your wagon, but I find myself much better off on your horse."

The wagoner, who now knew that Rübezahl had played him a trick, ran to the nearest village, told the people of his adventure with the Mountain Lord, and requested the landlord of the inn to lend him horses to bring his wagon to Hirschberg. The man willingly complied, and accompanied him with many others who wanted to witness the affair with their own eyes.

As they approached the wagon they heard a cheerful neighing and saw the remaining horse standing erect, pawing the ground with his forefeet as if to greet his master. Fresh and in good condition, the horse stood there and seemed only to await orders to set the wagon in motion. The wagoner was delighted that at least one horse was left, and he did his best to forget the loss of the other.

From that time the sulky wagoner became friendly and pleasant to everyone. There was always a seat for any old woman or fatigued traveler that he chanced to meet on the road. "For," he would say to himself, "who knows but it may be Rübezahl again?"

TAILOR ZWIRBEL

IN ORDER TO TEST the honesty of the tailor guild, Rübezahl, with a bundle of the finest cloth under his arm, wandered one day to Landeshut to order a court costume. As he nowhere perceived a tailor's sign, he approached a well from which a maiden was drawing water and asked where a tailor could be found. She politely told him that in the large corner house nearby lived Leberecht Zwirbel, the best known tailor in town. It was he who made clothes for the burgomaster, the clergyman, and other respectable people. The Mountain Spirit thanked her and went directly to the house she had pointed out.

He entered the workroom where twelve apprentices handled needles and shears as busily as if they'd to clothe a regiment of hussars. They barely looked up when Rübezahl entered the room. The worthy master Leberecht Zwirbel stood at the ironing board, pressing a coat ornamented with silver lace, to which he was giving the finishing touches. Quickly he laid his work aside when the stranger entered. Rübezahl's fine coat, cut in the latest fashion, impressed Zwirbel greatly. He welcomed the visitor with much courtesy and humbly asked what Rübezahl desired.

"My good master," answered Rübezahl, "I have

heard of your skill as a tradesman. I wish to know whether you can have a garment, such as Polish noblemen wear, made by next Sunday. I want one richly adorned with heavy cord and gold buttons. I have been invited to a banquet over the border, and I wish to dress in Polish costume. Saturday evening my servant will call for the garment and at the same time pay the bill. I wear nothing that has not been paid for. You will, I know, take pains to make the coat as fine and becoming as possible.

If I'm satisfied with your work, it will be to your advantage for my wealthy friends will want to know your name and they will, no doubt, honor you with orders. Here is the material. You have rarely had such fine cloth under your shears."

At these words he opened his bundle. Smirking, the tailor twisted and turned and patted the expensive material.

"You're right, noble sir," he said; "I have seldom handled such cloth, and I promise you that the work shall praise the master. Without boasting, I can assure you that I'm the best known tailor in all Silesia,

> For Zwirbel, the tailor,
> throughout the wide land,
> By young and by old
> is in constant demand.

You may inquire with the distinguished ladies and gentlemen of the neighborhood. They all know me. Many of my customers are princes, noblemen, clergy and the devout. Many rich men come to me for style because, as the proverb says, 'Clothes make the man.' I firmly believe that if Rübezahl had had a coat made by me, the beautiful Emma would have accepted him and Prince Ratibor would have been the disappointed one."

At these words he laughed merrily, for he felt that he had made a good joke. With many bows and apologies he proceeded to take his new customer's measurements. Meanwhile Rübezahl turned to the apprentices and asked about their journeyman travels. Then he asked if they'd ever met the Mountain Lord.

"With that sly chap," said one of them, "no ordinary man can cope." With this all the others agreed. "Take good care," continued the first speaker, "that you have nothing to do with him."

During this chat master Zwirbel had unrolled the cloth. He stretched it now this way, now that, and shook his head doubtfully. With much wrinkling of his face, he put on and took off his great horn-rimmed spectacles as if thinking carefully. The stranger looked sidewise at the actions of the cunning tailor and finally asked him why he looked so concerned. Master Zwirbel scratched thoughtfully behind his ears and said, "You have hardly brought me enough cloth, noble sir, to make the Polish coat you want."

Rübezahl knew right well that there was plenty for his purpose and to spare. However, he merely said in an annoyed tone, "Then the cloth merchant erred and must have cut off too little. Do your best with what you have. Perhaps, after all, you can get enough for my Polish coat."

Leberecht Zwirbel assured him on his honor as a tailor that he would deal honestly by him and would use every inch to the best advantage. He accompanied the distinguished looking gentleman to the door, and with many bows hoped to have the honor of seeing him again.

"There's a rich morsel for me," smirked the tailor as he snapped his fingers at the departing customer. "I shall charge well for the coat and I can keep at least two yards of the expensive material."

At the appointed time a servant wearing a fine uniform came and paid for the coat in bright silver pieces. Zwirbel inquired very anxiously concerning the name and residence of his master. The servant answered, disdainfully, "Do you know so little of the nobility, of the richest landowner in Silesia, of the count Rübenfeld of Riesenstein?"

With these words he went his way, leaving the tailor sunk in deep thought and striving in vain to recall the name he had just heard.

Autumn was at hand. The mildness of the Old Wife's summer was felt in the hazy atmosphere. On field and plain, on shrub and tree, floated filmy gossamers, that glanced in the sunlight like a silver net.

Worthy master Zwirbel, with his apprentices, rambled one fine Sunday toward the mountains to climb the Schneekoppe and pass a pleasant day there. Once a year it was his custom to turn his back on his gloomy workroom, to forget all business cares and in the clear pure sunshine dust away the cobwebs from his brain. The little company was well provided with refreshments, and the apprentices took turns carrying a well-filled basket laden with white bread, ham, sausages, roast fowl, and several bottles of red wine.

Just as the merry picnickers almost reached the summit, a huge white goat with immense horns suddenly came toward them. On his back sat a strange-looking rider, clad in a scarlet doublet, knee breeches and black shiny boots with red tops and silver buckles and a black silk cap with a white feather. To his terror, master Zwirbel, who led the party, recognized the rider as the distinguished gentleman for whom he had made the Polish coat. He at once realized that he had stolen a couple of yards of expensive cloth from no less a person than Rübezahl himself.

"Welcome, noble master," said the rider mockingly, "welcome to my domain. I have long had a desire to thank you for the finely made Polish coat, as well as for the modesty with which you treated yourself. I'll now settle with you over the two yards of cloth which you have thrown away, accidentally, of course, into a corner of your miserable shop; for

> From the top of your head
> to the soles of your feet,
> My dear master Zwirbel,
> you're naught but a cheat."

The terrified tailor saw at once that lying would be of no use. He fell on his knees, raised his hands imploringly, and whimpered, "Have pity, mighty ruler of the Riesengebirge! Let mercy take the place of justice. I solemnly promise never again to appropriate an inch of my customers' goods. If ever you find a shred of stolen cloth in my shop, you can roast me alive on the gridiron in your glowing furnace."

"Well," said Rübezahl, "if I treated you like you do others, I would cast you down my smoking chimney; but I shall be merciful and inflict a very mild punishment. Mount this horned and bearded friend in my place and, as knight of the goat, enter the town through the Landeshuter gate and ride to the door of your own house."

The worthy master was red with shame as he thought how the troublemaking children would run after him, shouting and shrieking; him, the honorable Leberecht Zwirbel, who, with his straight back and silver-headed cane, had always walked so majestically through the town! He trembled at the thought and began to speak it, but the malicious Mountain Spirit lost patience. With sinewy arm he grasped the insignificant little tailor by the neck, held him in the air till the writhing culprit shrieked in terror, and then set him on the goat's back.

Rübezahl then turned to the trembling apprentices and said, "Since none of you would have anything to do with me, you honorable members of an honorable guild, I shall have something to do with you. Grasp tightly the shaggy coat of the horned horse so that you can make your ride through the air without danger. All of you together don't weigh much, and you will be but a very light load for such a powerful steed."

As Rübezahl spoke, the journeymen were drawn to the goat like iron filings to a magnet. They were forced to grasp his shaggy coat and hang on for dear life. After all of the apprentices were hanging to the goat's coat, Rübezahl said to Master Zwirbel in threatening tones, "Should you ever again yield to temptation and cheat your customers, the goat will be at your door immediately and he'll bring you at once to my furnace. I earnestly advise you against being my guest. You would sigh in vain to be back to your needle and shears."

A shrill whistle was heard, followed by a burst of mocking laughter which the ravines and hollows threateningly echoed. Like a balloon the goat rose slowly in the air with the tailor and his companions. He then shot forward like an arrow. At the Landeshuter gate he descended. The apprentices felt their hands suddenly freed from the magnetic force which held them and they fell off like ripe plums from a tree, but luckily reached the ground in safety.

Leberecht Zwirbel sat on the animal's back as if he were strapped there. He tried to dismount, but in vain. He couldn't move, and he was obliged to make his triumphal entry into the town on the goat's back, shouted at and surrounded by the Landeshuter rabble. Dripping with perspiration he reached his dwelling.

As if at the word of command, the goat stopped before the door. At last, the tailor was able to free himself from the goat. He dismounted, rushed into the house and locked the door behind him. Just then came a flash of lightning, and the crowd, looking about, noticed that the goat had disappeared.

Master Zwirbel kept his word. He became the most

conscientious of tailors. The number of customers who flocked to his shop increased greatly. He never repented his goat ride. "For," he said, when speaking about it, "through that ride, I realized that after all, 'Honesty is the best policy'."

Rübezahl was ready at all times to help the needy and deserving, though he was feared because of his many vicious pranks. He was justly dreaded by the avaricious and the dishonest. As a rule, one lesson from the mighty Mountain Lord was enough to bring about a genuine reformation. Tailor Zwirbel's adventure was often referred to by the people as an evidence of this.

THE FLUTE PLAYER

FOR CENTURIES the great country of Bohemia had been the land of wandering musicians. These with harp, flute, clarinet or violin, travelled everywhere, playing for the evening dance or the summer festival, and they were always welcome visitors in town and hamlet.

From time out of mind they attended the great fair at Leipzig, and many were the silver pieces which they carried back to their distant homes. The rich merchants were especially generous to them, as their sprightly music often brought customers to their shops.

There was a flute player named Claus, and he had gotten considerably skilled with his instrument. On the Leipzig trip he traveled with some other musicians, but stood out amongst them for his genial manners. His playing was often generously rewarded.

After the great fair, Claus and his companions traveled through Saxony and Silesia on their return journey to Prague. In the villages along the main road they usually stayed one or more days playing for willing listeners. In this way they defrayed their current expenses so they could make it home without lessening what they'd earned at Leipzig.

At one of the villages they found that the harvest

gathering had called everyone old and young to the fields. There was a deathlike stillness everywhere; no inquisitive maidens peeped from the windows; no merry fellows called out a welcome to them. At the best, a frightened cat ran across the road, or a flock of disturbed sparrows flew in the air.

The tired musicians went to the village inn, refreshed themselves with a frugal meal, crossed their arms on the table and wearily let their heads sink on them. All except Claus were soon asleep. He thought of his return home and of his future after he had reached there; also of his vain efforts so far to earn enough to marry his beloved Anna, his betrothed.

He only made a little money flute playing back home in Prague and when Anna became his cherished wife, he could no longer pass his days on the high road to earn a livelihood. His greatest wish was to remain at home and live in peace and contentment.

All these thoughts passed actively through his mind. He wondered how he could find a way to enable him to have a peaceful, steady occupation. Suddenly, one of his companions awoke and said laughingly, "I have just seen Rübezahl in a dream. He might meet us on our travels, for we are approaching the haunted Riesengebirge."

To Claus these words sounded like the voice of destiny. He now knew to whom he should turn. Rübezahl had often helped needy, deserving persons, and would, he hoped, not fail to come to his assistance. He decided to part from his companions at once and set out by himself to the mountains.

Meanwhile the day had almost passed. The evening bells[4] rang peacefully in the valley. The harvesters, men, women, and children, were returning with blue cornflowers decorating their scythes and rakes. Heavily laden wagons drove into the open

---

[4] Per text: vesper bells, which are evening church bells

barns. The village seemed to come awake, and bustling life was everywhere to be seen. The musicians, playing lustily, proceeded to the village linden, where there was soon assembled a crowd, eager for the dance. The well-fed sheriff with his stately wife led the march, and in fullness of mirth and joy one pair after another joined in the dance.

As the dancers were whirling about at their wildest, Claus, flute in hand, slipped quietly away. No one noticed his absence, for all were merry with the harvest festivities. The moon shone brightly and lighted the wanderer's path. In the distance the Riesengebirge loomed aloft like a haunted shadow. The flute player knew no fear. Nothing but expectant hope filled his breast. He bravely continued through the night. In the morning as the church bells of a neighboring village were ringing, he found himself at the foot of the mountains and vigorously bent his steps upward.

He went that for some time and was about to rest awhile, when he saw a distant an open lawn and a beautiful mansion. As Claus had heard much of Rübezahl and his magical powers, he concluded that this castle was one of the many tricks of the powerful Mountain Lord who was, for the time being, undoubtedly residing there. He fearlessly stepped before the grated door and made ready to play.

A distinguished looking, richly-clad gentleman came out. His violet-blue satin coat was adorned with the costliest lace. Beautiful rings, which glittered like dewdrops in the sunshine, adorned his white slender fingers. He asked the startled Claus what his wishes were. The latter answered in tremulous tones that he had come there to give an exhibition of his flute playing.

"If you can play something really excellent," said the gentleman kindly, "you're welcome, for I'm passionately fond of good music."

A strange anxiety now seized the poor musician. If his playing didn't meet with Rübezahl's approval, he was lost. In his mind he saw himself hanging on a near-by tree as a punishment for his presumption. But it was too late for hesitation; he had to play even at the risk of his life. He who dares something may always hope to win something.

Claus exerted his utmost skill to please his listener, and he felt that he had never played better. Still he worried whether Rübezahl was pleased with his efforts. He awaited the decision of the owner of the castle.

Rübezahl, who had listened attentively, blew a beautiful silver whistle. The trembling musician believed his last hour had come and feared each moment that a gnome would rise out of the earth and drag him to the underworld. Instead, however, a beautiful young man appeared with a golden flute whose brilliancy dazzled the eye.

Seating himself on the edge of a marble basin, in the center of which was a fountain, he began to play. Claus had never heard the tune before. Like an angel's voice the flute sounded in soft, melting notes. Claus trembled and forgot everything in his delight.

The gentleman asked him, "What do you think of the music?"

"Ah, sir! I'm ashamed that I assumed so much about my wretched playing. Kindly forgive me and let me go my way."

"'Tis well," answered Rübezahl, "that you realize your music was only bungling. Return to your home and learn your instrument better. When you have improved, you can let me hear you again. As a memento you may take this golden flute, which seems to give you so much delight."

With these words he took the instrument from the beautiful youth and handed it to the astonished Claus. There was no end to Claus's thanks, and he promised tireless practice in his art to make himself worthy of the costly gift. He bade farewell to the kindly Mountain Spirit and started joyfully homeward.

On his return to Prague he practiced with unwearied zeal on his golden flute. Through his efforts it acquired more and more the musical tones that had enchanted him on the lawn of Rübezahl's castle. Finally he became a renowned artist and no longer had to play at fairs and markets. He earned in Prague a more than comfortable livelihood and was soon able to marry his beloved Anna.

Whether he ever again visited the Riesengebirge to serenade the Mountain Lord the story does not say. He may have done so, enabling Rübezahl to rejoice over mankind's gratitude

THREE STUDENTS

ONE BEAUTIFUL SPRING MORNING three merry students were strolling along the road outside of Prague, famous for its university, singing loudly:

"Now, May is come, the trees in bloom are
budding once again,
Who so desires, with restless care, may safe
at home remain ;
As clouds, in Heaven's azure vault, roam
restless here and there,
So we shall wander, joyful, round this world
of ours so fair."

They were going Silesia to spend the holidays with relatives. As they didn't have a lot of money they traveled on foot, and in many a home they found free lodging. They were easily satisfied so they were gladly received everywhere, and in student fashion they played many a cheerful hoax.

On the third day they reached the Riesengebirge. They longed for the freedom that exists on the mountains. If they were only on the heights! But the road was steep and the sun was burning hot.

One of them, named Thomas, finally asked, "What do you think, comrades? Shall we find any refreshment on the hills?"

"I hardly think so," answered Gottfried. "When my

landlord in Prague described the road over the mountains, he said we could wander for many miles without seeing a house. Rübezahl, the Lord of the Mountains, suffers no inn on his special territory."

"Ah! Your landlord is a humbug," said Paul. "It is over thirty years since he traveled this road. In that time what changes may not have happened? After all, the Mountain Lord might build himself an inn just for the pleasant company of jovial travelers."

"Indeed," said Gottfried, "it would be nothing for him to conjure an inn even in the dreariest wilderness."

"You surely don't believe that," said Thomas. "You certainly place no credibility in the Rübezahl fictions. Our professors down below taught us differently."

Paul also ridiculed Gottfried because of his belief in Rübezahl, but the student maintained that even here on the dreary Riesengebirge the Mountain Spirit could easily erect an inn should the fancy seize him.

"It wouldn't be such a bad thing," joked Paul, "if we found something to eat and drink here, and I shall give my sincere thanks to Rübezahl."

"Stop talking foolish," answered Gottfried. "It wouldn't be the first time that the Mountain Lord silenced someone like you as well as playing a vicious prank on him."

Talking this way they found themselves on the mountain ridge, and behold! close by the road was a cheerful-looking inn with a bowling alley in the adjoining field. A portly innkeeper in his shirt sleeves stood at the open door. The students greeted him joyfully, for an inn amid the mountain wastes was as welcome as a stream in the desert.

The innkeeper greeted them, removing his velvet cap, and said, "You will almost certainly rest awhile and refresh yourselves before traveling on. With what can I serve you?"

"I think, Mr. Landlord," said Paul as they all

entered, "before we order it would be well to tell us what you have. I don't suppose your menu will have a lot to choose from."

"Just give your order, gentlemen," said the host. "Kitchen and cellar are at your disposal."

"In that case," said Paul, "bring three roast pigeons with salad, a plate of nicely boiled crabs, some roast lamb and vegetables and coffee and dessert."

Hereupon the students went to the dining room, laid aside their packs, and made themselves comfortable while the host put his larder in requisition to fill their order. After a short while the innkeeper returned, spread a white cloth on the table, set knives and forks, and brought the meal.

While he was arranging the dishes he said, "Pigeons are rather scarce up here just now. Consequently they're somewhat dear; also the crabs, which are barely in season. These are the first caught this year. But, gentlemen, I hope you think as the proverb says, 'Nothing is too good for one's appetite,' although I know that a student often feels his stomach heavier than his purse."

"With your leave," said Thomas, "whether the stomach or the purse pinches a student most is the student's business, and it is not anyone else's concern."

"Now, young sir, don't take me so seriously. If the joke was not well received, it was at least well meant. Now, good appetite to you all." While the students were enthusiastically eating, the innkeeper placed a chair by the window, put on his glasses and began to read.

"What are you reading, landlord?" asked Gottfried. "If it's a religious book you can tell me about it. I understand such matters quite well, as I study theology at the University."

"See, young man," said the host, "this book holds a lot of valuable information good for everyone, whether theologian, lawyer, or doctor, to know. It begins this way: 'Be sensible and don't overload your stomach with dainties which bring discomfort; be content with nourishing, healthy and simple food; for what is beyond the ordinary costs usually causes illness.'"

"Do you again taunt us?" Paul burst out angrily, "and do you think we relish the biting pepper you're gave us to taste? Keep your book wisdom for yourself, and don't insist on showing it as if we were school children you have to teach good manners to. We get enough of that at the university and have no need to hear it at an inn table."

"Don't fly up to the roof, young sir," answered the host. "You entirely misunderstand me and take everything too much to heart. Enjoy your meal, for it pleases the host best when his guests eat heartily."

As the innkeeper now left the room, the three comrades looked at one another and in whispers debated whether the bill would be more than they could pay. Gottfried said that he believed the host was the Mountain Lord himself, who, he was sure, wouldn't charge them too much. The others laughed aloud and told him his childish belief would fade away.

"Just wait," said Paul, "until the innkeeper presents his bill. He probably knows accounting very well[5]." Gottfried was about to say something in support of his view and in favor of the host when the latter entered with the dessert.

Gottfried, who until now had been silent and dreamy, became merry and talkative. He clapped the innkeeper confidentially on the shoulder and invited him to join them in a toast. The innkeeper modestly declined, saying it was not proper for him to mingle with the young gentlemen, but the good-natured student insisted.

"I shall propose a health," he said, "and you must

---

[5] Per original text: "understands the art of writing with double chalk"

join."

Finally the innkeeper agreed. Gottfried cleared his throat like a professor about to deliver a lecture to his students, and in a grave voice said: "It appears almost like magic to find an inn so well furnished here on the summit of the Riesengebirge, far from the haunts of men the great highways. We were reliably informed that no shelter of this kind could be found far or near. For this happy circumstance we are indebted to the Lord of the Mountains. Let us therefore give him a grateful 'Good Health'."

Saying this he clinked glasses with his host. The others followed his example and cried loudly, "Hurrah for Rübezahl!"

The host made a wry face and seriously said, "Your friend has done honor to the Lord of the Mountains and I joined with him. You, however, called him by his mock name. I can't join that sentiment, for nothing makes him angry like reminding him of his unhappy love affair."

The two merry comrades laughed, scorning this warning. Their jolly mood couldn't be readily disturbed, and if the severe rector of the Prague University had suddenly appeared at the open door, they would have fallen joyously on his neck.

"How, now," said they. "Why should we worry about the Mountain Lord? Who or what is he? A mere fancy of the brain, a belief that exists only in spinning rooms when maidens scare each other with ghost stories. We of the Prague University are not so simple as to believe such nursery tales. Brother Gottfried alone has preserved his childish faith in such things; but we disciples of the law and of medicine say with one voice, 'Out with the bugbear! Away with Rübezahl!'"

The host was undecided whether to laugh or to give a sound thrashing to the daring fellows.

As he looked, however, at their happy faces he

said to himself, "It's their foolish youth talking, and I'm well aware that they mean no harm."

Suddenly he said to the merry crowd, "How would a game of bowling please you? It's good exercise after a meal and will sober you up. The alley is new and the balls roll perfectly true."

The students agreed. The innkeeper volunteered to be the alley boy and the game began. Gottfried rolled the first ball. It went straight on, and struck the king pin fairly in the middle. He repeated this master stroke twice in a row. Thomas, surprised, tried to follow his example but he had hardly rolled when the ball swerved here and there and at last jumped clear of the king as if it had nothing to do with the game. When Paul rolled his ball, it did the same thing.

After they'd rolled several games they were frustrated and decided to stop playing.

Now came the most serious part of the merry feast. It was time to pay the bill, and they didn't have a lot of money. In an embarrassed tone and with downcast eyes, Thomas asked for the amount of the bill. The host laughed to himself as he saw how humble the formerly haughty fellow had become.

"You, my dear sir," said he, turning to Gottfried with a polite bow, "owe nothing. Your bowling has paid your bill. I take nothing from a guest who once makes the king, and you did it three times. Of course the other gentlemen must pay a dollar each."

The two looked at each other, satisfied, for they'd expected the charge would be higher. They took out their purses and cheerfully paid the money, which was the exact amount they'd.

At parting the host gave to each a neatly wrapped little package. He said, "You must now travel the entire day before you come to another inn. It helps to have a bite handy when Mr. Stomach starts to pinch, for he is a persistent fellow who will not be put off with promises. To you, young gentleman," addressing Gottfried, "as a memento, I present the king from the bowling alley. Hold him in esteem and allow nothing to keep you bringing him safely home."

He bowed politely to his guests. They cheerfully departed, for they'd been well entertained and the charges had been very moderate.

The students traveled many miles without seeing a habitation. Finally Thomas said to his friends, "The roast pigeons and the boiled crabs have not lasted long. My stomach is growling like a hungry wolf. Let's eat the lunch our host so considerately gave us. You, Gottfried, can now and then take a bite of your bowling king as you have nothing else to eat."

Gottfried laughed at their jesting, and answered, "Eat heartily. I shall not deprive you of your portions, for I'm not hungry. Since I never thoughtlessly throw away a gift I shall bring my king home, although it feels pretty heavy."

The others took from their pockets the neatly wrapped sandwiches. As they opened the packages, they let them fall in horror to the ground, for a big, long-legged frog jumped out of each. The two alert students realized they'd been tricked and would complained about the innkeeper, but they remembered they were still in the Mountain Spirit's domain. They were now convinced that their landlord had been none other than Rübezahl himself. They were glad that a harmless fright was the only evil consequence of their rashness.

Meanwhile, night had fallen and the weary travelers could barely see their way. Suddenly the king which Gottfried faithfully carried under his arm began to glitter and gradually spread a light as bright as a lantern.

This fact didn't shock the students; they'd seen so many wonders within a few hours and were now so thoroughly careful of every word and action that they all patiently waited till later for an explanation of the strange occurrence.

When they reached the Silesian side of the mountains and had arrived at the town where their relatives resided, they examined the bowling king to figure out why it glowed. To their surprise it was pure gold.

"See," said Gottfried to his companions, "how the Lord of the Mountains has rewarded me because I didn't, like you, mock and insult him."

LITTLE PETER

LITTLE PETER was a little boy with curly hair that lived in the village of Krummhübel at the foot of the Schneekoppe. His father was a woodchopper in the near-by forest. He would go to work in the early morning and returned late in the evening. Peter's mother was dead and the household cares were managed by Peter's aunt.

She was very strict over the motherless boy, whose never failing cheerfulness annoyed her. She had no patience with the loud, active lad. He jumped and sprang around like a grasshopper, and sang cheerily as a lark. The malicious old aunt, for that matter, didn't like children. She couldn't understand their little joys and sorrows. She scolded, pushed and buffeted little Peter all day long.

There was neither peace nor joy for him at home; but in the open he found friends everywhere. Colored butterflies flittered about him, the beetles whirred and droned and the larks trilled. The cuckoo played hide and seek with him and cried mockingly, "Cuckoo!" Peter would look around but could never find the mischievous bird. "Ah!" he would cry angrily, "I can't see you. I only wish I couldn't see the cross aunt at home any more. She doesn't cares about me and she is only happy when I'm out of her sight."

One day the aunt was expecting a visit from a

young relative. In honor of her guest, she bought a fine trout which she put into a tub of water to keep it alive.

"Poor animal," said Peter, as he saw the fish, "you would rather swim in a large pool than find yourself in this narrow place. Come, I'll give you your freedom."

So saying he took the flopping fish out of the water and brought it to the brook that flowed near the house. The trout, rejoicing in its freedom, splashed about, beat the water with its tail, made little ripples, and joyfully darted here and there over the white shining pebbles. Peter looked with delight at this merry sport and sprang joyfully around on one leg.

His happiness was suddenly ended by a blow on his ear which, he soon realized, came from the bony hand of his aunt.

"You worthless booby," she screamed; "what kind of a trick have you played on me? Wait till your father comes home; he'll take care of you. What do I feed your cousin since kitchen and cellar are empty?"

Peter worried he did wrong. He begged his aunt to forgive him; he had meant no harm, and it was only out of pity that he had set the trout free. It was no use and that evening, after receiving the promised punishment from his father, he went sorrowfully to bed.

Despite how bad he felt, sleep soon closed his weary eyes. A pleasant dream led him through the woods and showed him so many beautiful things that, next morning, he woke up in a cheerful mood and ate his breakfast as happily as ever.

Just as he was about to go outside like usual, his aunt called him back and screamed harshly, "You lazy bones, you're big enough to help out around here. Your father became sick during the night and can't go to work today. Go to the wheat fields and glean. Don't return until you have filled this bag."

She gave him a large sack, and poor Peter slunk

sadly away to work. At the first field he came to, other more industrious gleaners had been there before him. All they had left were scattered ears of grain here and there. He wandered from one field to another, but everywhere he came too late. Noon was long past, evening was fast approaching, and his sack was not even half filled. The poor fellow began to cry resentfully; he sat down, tired and unhappy.

Suddenly there stood before him an old hunter who asked in a friendly tone why he was weeping. Peter, encouraged by his kind manner, told him all his woes and how his aunt tortured him and was angry when he sang. The hunter, full of sympathy, heard his complaints and asked, "What do you really wish should happen to your aunt as punishment? Shall I put a lock on her wicked mouth to keep her from scolding you? Shall I stop up her ears so she can't hear? Shall I break one leg off short so she can't chase you and beat you? Tell me your wish and I'll quickly punish her."

"Ah! no, sir," answered the boy. "Don't hurt my aunt or in the end she'll be worse than ever. Oh! If I only knew where I could find enough wheat to fill my big sack."

"Well," said the hunter as he kindly laid his hand on Peter's curly head, "I'll help you quickly."

He put his finger to his mouth and whistled shrilly. Swiftly a flock of sparrows appeared and descended like a dark cloud on the stubble field. The diligent little birds found the stray ears and brought them together in a heap. When this was large enough the hunter said, "My son, you may get to work; I think you now have plenty to fill your sack."

Peter did as he was told. When he turned to thank his unknown helper, the latter had disappeared.

Only his friends, the sparrows, were there, and these with joyful twitter accompanied him on his way home. At the house door Peter stood as if in a dream and looked at the birds that had perched on the trees in the adjoining garden.

All he had gone through seemed wonderful— the strange hunter, the tiny bird gleaners; and the well-filled sack had been so light he hardly felt the weight! The scolding voice of the aunt finally woke him from his dream. "You sluggard," she screamed, "where have you been rambling so long? Did you need an entire day to gather these few ears?"

This scolding didn't bother Peter; he could now exchange his wheat for corn meal at the mill.

Next morning, after he had eaten his sparse breakfast, his aunt ordered him to catch a mess of fish for his father. "Don't come back with empty hands," she called after him.

Peter took his net from the wall, went out and sat under a willow by the neighboring brook and dipped his net into the merrily splashing water. Hours passed, noon came, but his net was still empty. Much discouraged, the young fisherman leaned against the trunk of the willow, and his eyes, which usually sparkled with merriment, filled with big tears. He saw himself unable to catch the fish his father wanted. He looked eagerly down the valley to see if his old friend would return once more to help him. Just then the hunter's athletic form came out of the shadow of the wood and he walked to the spot where Peter sat.

"Ah! sir," Peter called to him, "Please help me to catch some fish, or my father will have no dinner today, and, besides, my aunt will half kill me."

"Poor boy," was the answer, "have you caught nothing yet? Then I must help you."

He whistled, but more lightly than on the previous day. A large trout appeared in the water, driving before him a shoal of small fish that swam into the net. There were so many fish that Peter was able to empty the net twice. He shouted for joy at the fortunate catch, and the hunter looked kindly at the merry youngster.

"That's enough now," said Peter. "All three at home can have a real feast. Master hunter, won't you kindly be our guest so that my father may thank you ?"

"Many thanks for your invitation," smilingly answered the old man. "If I don't accept today, I certainly shall some other time. But see! Look at that big trout. Don't you know him? He is an old acquaintance of yours. You were once his benefactor. You took him out of the narrow tub and gave him his freedom. Today he has repaid your kindness."

Much surprised, Peter looked at the fish as he peacefully swam here and there in the brook, looking up from time to time as if to say, "Yes, indeed, I know you." As Peter turned to the hunter he found that the latter had disappeared again. The boy joyfully hurried home with his rich catch. The sick father feasted on the dainty food and praised Peter for his skill.

Next morning Peter thought, "Today I'll remain at home with my father." But his aunt came and shouted in her harsh tones, "Get ready at once and go to the mountains. When you get there call for Rübezahl. If he appears, beg him for some gopher plant[6] for your sick father. He'll die if you don't get some, as there is no other help for him. Stay in the mountains until Rübezahl hears you and grants your request. If you return without the gopher plant, it will be your fault if your father dies."

"He'll certainly never return," murmured the wicked-minded old woman. "Rübezahl will hang him on the nearest tree or hurl him down to the underworld for calling him by his nickname."

Peter put a piece of black bread in his pocket, took a stick that he had cut from a blackthorn and started vigorously in the direction of the near-by mountains. He was familiar with the many alarming tales about the powerful Mountain Spirit. He had heard them

---

[6] springwurzel, per original text

related on fine summer evenings when the young men and maidens told old folk tales sitting under the linden tree. But he was not at all afraid. People told just as much good about Rübezahl that he pictured him as a kind old gentleman who would do a little boy no harm.

Peter was, therefore, in a cheerful mood. The fresh sunny morning, the singing birds, the green woods and the lofty mountains, all agreed with his mood. Fearlessly he climbed the steep, rugged paths. When he had nearly reached the summit, he rested awhile to get his breath so that his cry of "Rübezahl!" would resound clearly through the mountain air. He had opened his mouth as wide as he could and was about to shout, when suddenly a hand was laid upon his shoulder and a well-known voice asked, "What are you doing here so early in the wild mountains, little Peter?"

"Thank God!" cried the boy joyfully as he recognized the kind-hearted hunter. "I now feel safe since you're with me. My aunt has ordered me to call Rübezahl and to beg him for some gopher plant to make father well."

"But are you not afraid of the terrible Mountain Spirit?" asked the hunter.

"Ah! no," answered Peter. "The Spirit punishes people that mock him, but he surely wouldn't hurt a little child who begs for his sick father."

"You may be right," agreed the hunter, "but who knows if he would hear your call? Perhaps he is traveling in some other part of his dominions and before he returns your father might die. We hunters, however, know all the roots and herbs in the mountains for we go everywhere, in caves, ravines, and chasms. In this way I once found the celebrated gopher plant. I'll give you some. Scrape it very fine and have your father eat it."

Little Peter wished to give a thankful 'God reward you' to the friendly hunter but the latter had stepped forward slowly through the long grass and dense undergrowth. He turned about once and merrily waved his green felt hat with the beautiful eagle's feather before proceeding towards the Schneekoppe. To the wondering Peter he appeared taller and taller, until his head seemed to reach a passing white cloud in which his entire form at last vanished.

To the spirited lad all this appeared very strange. Then he thought of his father, and holding the gopher plant firmly in his hand, he ran down the mountain to his home.

He went quickly to his sick father and told him of his strange meetings with the powerful Mountain Spirit. The father listened eagerly to the tale of little Peter.

Peter scraped the gopher plant according Rübezahl's directions and gave some to his father. Next day when the sick man awoke he had thoroughly recovered.

From that time the wicked aunt who had embittered the boy's life stopped being unkind to him. Peter led a happy life, helped his father at his work and later became an industrious man who honorably supported himself by the work of his hands.

FARMER VEIT

A FARMER NAMED VEIT, having lost everything because of an unjust lawsuit, found himself reduced to poverty. Even his last cow had gone because of the legal decision, and nothing was left him but a sickly wife and a half dozen children. He was indeed industrious, and he had two sound, lusty arms, but these were not enough to support him and his family. It cut him to the heart when his children cried for bread and he had nothing with which to feed them.

"With a hundred dollars," he said to his careworn wife, "we could restore our ruined household, and we could buy new property far away from our law-seeking neighbor. You have wealthy relatives on the other side of the mountain. I'll go to them and tell them of our great need. Perhaps someone will take pity on us, and in pure goodness of heart will lend us at legal interest what we need."

The downhearted wife consented to this proposal, but she did not expect him to succeed.

Early next morning the farmer started his journey. As he parted from his family he inspired them with some of his own hope, saying, "Don't cry; my heart tells me I shall find a supporter who will help us." He put a piece of bread into his pocket as provision for the journey and went on his way.

Exhausted and almost overcome by the heat and

the long journey, he arrived that evening at the village where his in-laws lived. None of them wanted to know him; none of them would receive him into their home. With bitter tears he told them his troubles, but they were hard-hearted and pitiless. They overwhelmed the poor man with reproaches and insulting proverbs. One said, "Pride goes before a fall." Another, "As you manage so you thrive." A third, "Each man is the architect of his own fortune." So they shamed and mocked him, called him spendthrift and sluggard, and closed their doors in his face.

The poor farmer had not expected such a reception. Silently and sadly he slunk away, and as he had no money to pay for lodging, he passed the night in an open field in a haystack. Here he sleeplessly awaited the coming of day so he could go home.

On the way, he had to once again go through the Riesengebirge. When he found himself there, grief and despondency overcame him so much he was on the verge of despair. Weak from sorrow and hunger, without comfort, without hope, he stopped on the road.

He thought to himself, "Two days' wages lost for nothing. Now when you return and your six poor children look longingly for you, their hands stretched out, craving for food, you must give them a stone instead of bread. Father heart! How can you stand it? How can you witness such a sight!" Hereupon he threw himself in the shade of a tree to rest and wallow in his misery.

The soul on the verge of destruction often exercises its last strength to save itself. As a mariner who sees his ship sinking quickly climbs the mast to seek safety in the shrouds; or, if below, springs through the scuttle to secure a plank or an empty cask to keep himself afloat in the water, so came an inspiration to the unhappy Veit. In the midst of a thousand distracted thoughts the idea of appealing, in this his direst hour of need, to the mercy of the Mountain Lord suddenly struck him. He had heard many wonderful stories about this powerful Being; how at times he pestered and tormented travelers, playing many vicious tricks and inflicting malicious mischief, but at other times doing good. He also knew The Mountain Lord never allowed himself to be called by the mock name of Rübezahl without punishing those who did so. Nevertheless, in his despair, and as he didn't know any other way, Veit decided to risk it and he shouted with all his might "Rübezahl! Rübezahl!"

At this call a sooty workman appeared, armed with a huge poker, large as a weaver's beam, which he wrathfully flourished as if to kill the daring mocker. A long fox-red beard reached to his waist, and his enormous eyes were fiery and staring.

"With your favor, Rübezahl," said Veit, completely calm, "I beg your pardon for not naming you properly. I don't mean to insult you. I don't know your real name. Please listen to my story and then do with me as you will."

This courageous speech, and the troubled, careworn look of the man somewhat softened the wrath of the Mountain Spirit. "Earthworm," he spat, "what madness impels you to disturb me? Don't you know you must pay for your insult with your life?"

"Master," said Veit, "only the direst need sends me to you. I have a request which you can easily grant. Lend me a hundred dollars, and as certain as I'm an honest man I shall repay you with legal interest in three years."

"Fool!" said the Spirit, "Am I a banker to give out money on interest? Go to your fellow men and borrow from them as much as you need, and leave me in peace."

"Alas!" said Veit, "all is over between me and my fellow men. There is no longer any brotherhood between us."

He then told his pitiful story, and so touchingly pictured his bitter misery that Rübezahl couldn't refuse his request. The thought came to him that even if the fellow were less deserving of pity than he looked, this was a chance to gain a new and remarkable experience. He felt more than inclined to help poor Veit.

"Come, follow me," said Rübezahl. He led Veit through the woods to a distant valley, out of which rose a steep cliff whose base was hidden by a thick undergrowth. After Veit and his leader had pushed their way through with much difficulty, they were at the mouth of a gloomy cavern. The honest farmer didn't feel at all comfortable as he groped in the darkness. One shudder after another shook his frame, and his hair stood on end. He reflected that Rübezahl had often deceived others. What kind of abyss might lie ahead to fall into! At the same time he heard a mysterious rushing of waters like an underground stream in a deep mine.

The farther he went the more his heart beat with doubt and terror. Finally, to his great relief, he saw in the distance the flicker of a tiny flame. The cave gradually widened into a large roomy vault. The light, which now burned more brightly, was coming from a large lamp hanging from the rocky roof. On the floor he noticed a large copper pan filled to the brim with bright silver dollars. When Veit saw the treasure, all his terror disappeared and his heart leaped for joy.

"Take what you desire," said the Spirit, "be it much or little; but let me have a note for the amount, if you know how to write."

Veit assured him that he could write, and carefully counted out just one hundred dollars, no more, no less. The Spirit showed no interest, turned to one side and produced writing materials. The farmer drew up the note and made it as legally binding as he knew how. The Mountain Spirit locked the note in an iron safe and said, "My friend, go your way, and use your money with industry and thrift. Don't forget that you're my debtor. Remember the valley entrance as well as this rocky grotto. When the third year is over you're to pay me capital and interest. I'm a hard creditor, and if you don't make good your word, I shall get my own with violence, if necessary."

The trusty Veit, with a clasp of his honest hand, promised to make payment on the appointed day, but didn't, like many silly borrowers, pledge soul and salvation. With a thankful heart he left the rocky cavern, out of which he now readily found his way. The possession of the money worked so favorably on his mind and body that as he once more went into the cheerful light of day, he felt as if he had taken on a new life in Rübezahl's cave.

Full of joy, and strengthened in every limb, he headed straight for home. He got there by evening. When the children saw him they shouted together, "Bread, father, a piece of bread; we're almost starving." His wretched wife sat in a corner and wept. In her despair she feared the worst, knowing her hard-hearted relatives. She also feared that her husband, in the bitterness of disappointment, would take it out on her. But he greeted her cheerfully and directed her to make a fire on the hearth, for he had brought meat and bread from Reichenberg. The good wife soon prepared a nourishing dinner.

During the meal Veit told her of his success. "Your cousins," he lied, "are indeed worthy people. They didn't upbraid me with my poverty; they didn't disown me; neither did they drive me shamefully from their doors. They received me and entertained me generously. Their hearts and hands were open and they counted out a hundred dollars, which they cheerfully gave to me as a loan."

On hearing this, the heavy load that had long

oppressed his wife was lifted from her heart. "Had we gone to them sooner," she said, "we would have been spared much of our trouble." She boasted of her kinsmen, in whom she formerly had so little confidence, and acted as if she were proud of them.

Her husband purposely allowed her this gratification, pleasing her innocent vanity, as a way to make up for all she had been through. He finally became tired of her repeated praises and said to her, "When I was leaving your cousins, do you know the good advice they gave me? 'Each one,' they said, 'is the architect of his own fortune;' and 'One must strike the iron while it is hot.' Let us now turn to our work and apply ourselves so industriously that in three years we may be able to pay the loan with legal interest and be free from all debt."

Farmer Veit rented a meadow, and as he prospered from the beginning he was able to buy more and more land. Good fortune had come with Rübezahl's money, as if a magic multiplying dollar had been with it. Veit sowed and reaped, and he was soon regarded by his neighbors as a man well-to-do. His purse always contained money with which to broaden his purchases. By the third summer he had rented a large tract of land, which in addition to his little farm, brought him a considerable income. In short, he was now a man who prospered in every undertaking.

The time for settlement was finally at hand, and Veit found that he could pay his debt without difficulty or without being in any way inconvenienced.

One day he woke his wife and told her to prepare the children, to wash them, comb their hair, dress them in their Sunday clothes, and put on their new shoes. She was to wear her new skirt and her scarlet waist, which was also entirely new. Veit himself donned his best suit, and called to their servant Hans to harness the horses and get the wagon ready.

"Husband," said the wife, "what are you up to?

Today is neither a holiday nor a fair day. What makes you so cheerful? I feel you're giving us a pleasant surprise. Where do you intend to go ?"

He answered, "I intend to visit your relatives on the other side of the mountains, and I'm going to pay capital and interest to the tender-hearted creditors who helped me by their generous advances. Today is pay day." This greatly pleased his wife. She carefully dressed the children in their best, in order to impress her relatives with an idea of her prosperity, and in her innocent pride she put around her neck a string of pierced coins. Cheerfully rattling his heavy purse, Veit jumped into the wagon where his wife and children were already seated. Hans whipped up the horses, and all merrily started for the road that led to the Riesengebirge.

The route at first led through woods and dense undergrowth, and Veit's wife, supposing he had gone astray, suggested that he keep to the open road. After a while he left the wagon, gathered his wife and children around him, and said, "You think, dear wife, that we are going to your relatives, but nothing is farther from my thoughts. Your wealthy friends are misers and wretches. They mocked and abused me and mercilessly drove me away when I begged them in my poverty for help and support. The rich cousin to whom we owe our present prosperity lives here; the one who lent me, on the strength of my simple word, the money that has thrived so well in my hands. This is the day on which to pay him capital and interest. Do you not know now who our creditor is? He is the Lord of the Mountains, whom you know as Rübezahl!"

The wife was frightened at these words and crossed herself devoutly. The children trembled with terror, afraid their father would bring them to Rübezahl. They'd heard much about him in the spinning rooms, and had learned that he was a fearful giant and man-eater. Veit told them his whole story;

how the Mountain Spirit in the shape of a wood burner had appeared at his call; and what he had done for him in the cavern. With grateful heart and with warm tears running down his weather-beaten cheeks, he touchingly praised his benefactor's goodness.

"Wait here," he continued, "I'll now go to his cave and finish my business. Don't be afraid. I shall not be long, and if I can persuade the Mountain Spirit to come I shall bring him to you. Don't fear to shake his hand though it be black and sooty. He'll do you no harm, and most certainly will be as pleased at our heartfelt gratitude as at the happy result of his kindness. Be of good courage, children, he'll give you apples and ginger bread."

Although the terrified wife objected strongly, and the children, trembling and crying, gathered about their father and strove to draw him back, he forcibly broke away and entered the forest.

He arrived at the well-known rock and readily recognized all the landmarks. The old blasted oak, at whose roots the ravine began, was there as it had been three years before; but of the cave itself there was not the slightest trace. Veit sought in every possible way to find the entrance. He knocked with a stone on the rocks, which he thought would then open. He shook his heavy purse, rattled the silver dollars, and called out as loud as he could, "Mountain Spirit! Come receive what belongs to you." But the Spirit gave no sign, and the honest debtor at last saw that he would have to return with his obligation unpaid.

When his wife and children saw him coming they ran joyfully to meet him. He was dissatisfied and very much concerned at being unable to discharge his debt, and he sat on a grassy bank and reflected on what to do. He recalled his former rashness.

"I'll call the Mountain Lord by his mock name. Let him beat me if he wishes; he'll at least hearken to this call."

Then he shouted with all his might, "Rübezahl! Rübezahl!" The terrified wife bade him keep silence, but he only cried the louder, "Rübezahl! Rübezahl!"

Suddenly the youngest child ran to his mother and said in a frightened voice, "Ah! The black man!"

With much satisfaction Veit asked, "Where?"

"There he is, hiding behind that tree!"

The children huddled together, trembling with fright and crying piteously. The father looked, but saw no one; it must have been only the child's imagination; perhaps a shadow. Rübezahl didn't appear, and all calling was in vain.

The family started toward the main road where the wagon was in waiting. A gentle breeze coming from the depths of the forest swept through the trees. The tall birches nodded, the trembling aspen leaves fluttered and the rustling sounded closer and closer. Then came a strong wind which shook the mighty branches of the oaks, drove withered leaves and dry grass before it, and caused swirls of dust to rise on their path. This pleased the children greatly, and they no longer thought of Rübezahl.

They ran merrily after the dancing leaves driven here and there by the wind. The youngest chased after a piece of white paper which was whirled along among the leaves.

When he was about to grasp the paper, it was blown farther and farther away so that he couldn't catch it. He finally threw his hat after it and secured it. As it was a nice white sheet and the thrifty father used even the smallest trifles, the lad brought it to him expecting to be praised for his cleverness. Veit took the paper and saw that it was the identical note he had given Rübezahl three years before. It was torn across, and on it were the words, "Received payment, with thanks."

As he read these words Veit was deeply moved

and cried out joyfully, "Rejoice, dear wife and children; our gracious benefactor has seen us. Though invisible, he has hovered near us, and he knows that I'm an honest man. I have now discharged my obligations; we can contentedly return home."

Parents and children wept, but their tears were tears of happiness. On reaching the wagon, the wife expressed a desire to visit her relatives who had treated her good husband so pitilessly. They descended the mountain and by evening had reached the dwelling from which, three years before, Veit had been driven away so shamefully.

Although a humble, good-hearted, God-fearing man he couldn't help but feel pleased when he contrasted his present condition with that of three years before: now contented and happy; then heartbroken and on the verge of despair.

This time he knocked confidently and inquired after the owner. A man, not of his wife's kindred, answered. From him Veit learned that the rich cousins were no longer in the neighborhood. One was dead, another had failed, and a third had moved away.

Veit and his family remained overnight at the village inn. The friendly landlord related more fully the story of the wealthy relatives. Next day all returned home. Farmer Veit took up his work, increased his lands and riches, and remained a well-to-do farmer his lifelong.

THE HORSE DEALER

IN THE BOHEMIAN VILLAGE of Trautenau lived a horse dealer named Jacob. His great desire was to build up riches. In addition, he had a hard heart and no one could say that he had ever done a charitable act. He was a miser willingly suffered hunger and thirst just to save a few pennies. A herring with a piece of black bread served him for dinner, while a cup of wretched coffee was the only drink he ever allowed himself.

He went about dressed like a beggar. His coat was a medley of patches. You could hardly notice that it had once been black, for, like Joseph's coat, it was now of many colors. If a poor person asked him for alms he would whimper, "Oh, misery! I'm poor myself and have nothing in the world."

Yet he was rich, and he had sufficient means not only to lead a comfortable life but to be charitable as well. He had a strong box full of silver and gold over which he literally gloated when night came and every one had gone to sleep. He had dug out carefully beneath the floor of his hovel a hole just large enough to contain the box. Over this spot he regularly made his bed of straw and rags, and here he slept as peacefully as he could have done on a couch of down, for he knew that what was dearest to him on earth was perfectly safe.

He found his business, which consisted chiefly of

the sale and exchange of horses, very profitable. He was a cunning knave who knew how to trim and polish old worn-out horses, so that people thought they were young and faultless. Many a straightforward purchaser fell into his trap; for Jacob's appearance was such a picture of honesty that to have doubted him in any way seemed like a sin.

One day he was visited by a prosperous landowner of the neighborhood who desired to purchase six black and two white horses, for he was so rich that he could afford to ride eight-in-hand like a prince. A horse market was shortly to be held at Hirschberg, so he commissioned Jacob to make the purchase and gave him three thousand dollars for it. When the gentleman had gone, the dealer chuckled with pleasure. The transaction was likely to prove profitable and one that would easily yield him a few hundred for himself. He prepared to start for Hirschberg at once. He slung his wallet over his shoulder, took his thorn stick in his hand, and traveled the whole day in the dust and heat.

Toward evening he bent his steps to a wood and rested there for the night. He need pay nothing for this kind of lodging. Late on the second day he reached Hirschberg, sought an inn where many buyers and sellers put up, and slyly took note of all he saw and heard. He especially busied himself in the stalls, looked over and felt the horses, and was ready to appraise the value of each, for he thoroughly understood his business.

He went to the market early, and after buying six black horses and two white ones that were without a flaw, he found he had four hundred dollars left. For this sum he purchased a dapple gray which he calculated he could sell later for five hundred dollars.

He then set out for home. At first, everything went well. Jacob rode his own horse and led the others. Suddenly, his gray stood stock still and neither words nor blows could persuade him to move. The dealer was desperate, for he realized that the horse was balky, and that, clever as he was, he had been cheated by a rogue smarter than himself. After a quarter of an hour the horse went on, but shortly he stopped again and Jacob was obliged to wait patiently until the obstinate fit was over. He couldn't decide whether he should return to find the cheating horse dealer or go on his way.

Presently, he perceived in the distance a solitary farmhouse which he had not noticed on his way to the fair. He thought to himself, "I shall ask there for a night's lodging; perhaps the owner will give it to me for nothing." The dapple gray now ambling happily along with his black and white comrades brought his master without a break to the house where the owner stood in the open doorway. Jacob politely asked for a night's lodging for himself and horses and his request was cheerfully granted. He took the horses to the stable and then followed his host to the living room. As the farmer had no servants he, himself, brought soft black bread, fresh butter, and a glass of milk. These he set before his guest and invited him to partake freely of the simple meal.

After Jacob had refreshed himself, he talked about the lively doings at the Hirschberg market, and in boasting of his advantageous purchases he especially mentioned the dapple gray. He didn't speak, however, of the serious defect which rendered the horse useless for any practical purpose.

"The horse pleased me at first sight," said the farmer. "He is strong, well-built, and he has a beautiful color. I would have no objection to trade my brown for him. What do you say to this offer?"

At heart Jacob was delighted at the prospect of getting rid of his balky animal. Still he concealed his delight, looked very serious and answered, "I might accept your proposal, were it not that I'm greatly attached to that horse, and I would part from him with regret. Still, to show that I appreciate your hospitality, I'm willing to make the exchange provided you give me money to boot. Let us go to the stable to compare both animals, and you will readily see I'm making no unjust claim."

After the brown and the dapple gray had been thoroughly inspected, Jacob said to the farmer, "I know you don't wish me to be at a loss in this transaction. Give me your brown and a hundred dollars and I shall try to forget my dapple gray."

"The boot seems to me to be a little high," mused the farmer. "Still, as your horse pleases me, I'll accept your terms. I'm convinced from your honest appearance that you're selling me a horse free from any defect, sound in wind and limb. You have ridden him many miles and you must be able by this time to judge him correctly. Ask your conscience if you can answer for him; it would bring you no blessing should you succeed in overreaching me."

The horse dealer assured him that he couldn't act more honorably with his own brother. Upon returning to the house he received the hundred dollars with much satisfaction. He put the money in a leather belt which he wore around his waist. When his host finally suggested that he retire, he requested a few bundles of straw to make up a bed in the stable. He wished to disturb no one in the morning as it was his intention to start before sunrise.

"Your idea is a good one," said the farmer. "You will travel in the cool of the day and your horses will be less likely to be bothered with flies. I wish you a happy journey. My brown nag will take you safely home."

With a significant smile Jacob did not understand, the farmer directed him to take as much straw as he needed. His bed was soon ready and he lay down without undressing as he intended to start in a few hours. He worried the farmer might take a ride on the dapple gray in the early morning, or hitch him to a wagon, in which case he would be the loser, since he would be obliged to return the money and give up the brown.

The season was midsummer, when the nights are never very dark. Jacob noticed there was light enough to start two hours after midnight. He led the horses before the door, mounted the brown, took his line in hand and went forward in a gentle trot. The brown was all his master claimed; his step was light and sure and his rider felt not the slightest fatigue.

Meanwhile, day dawned, the cool morning air refreshed man and beast, and Jacob, since he had made a good bargain, was in the happiest frame of mind. He pictured the farmer sitting on the balky dapple gray, striving in vain to make him move. He couldn't refrain from laughing aloud.

Just then, in spite of the clear sky, a dark cloud lowered gradually over him, obscuring the blue heavens. He urged the horses to a faster pace but the cloud, still directly over his head, came nearer and nearer until it finally enveloped him and his horses. The cloud was really a huge mass of horseflies. They viciously bit both man and horses; the brown bucked and reared in anguish, threw his rider and then ran away at full gallop.

As Jacob recovered from the shock of the fall, and saw his six black and two white horses standing quietly on the road, he was satisfied that his punishment went no further than bruised and aching limbs. He recalled the farmer's meaning smile and his warning about the horseflies. He fully realized that the insect swarm had been sent by Rübezahl in revenge for the deceit that had been practiced on him in the horse bargain.

Jacob accepted his punishment as a lesson and was from that time forward an honest man.

THE BRAGGART'S PUNISHMENT

RÜBEZAHL IN THE GARB OF A HERMIT was one day strolling on the ridge of the Riesengebirge. He met a man who walked along with bowed head, and whose countenance bore every evidence that he was a confirmed drunk[7]. "What ails you, stranger?" said the Mountain Spirit in his accustomed way. "What is it you lack?"

"Everything but virtue," was the answer, "but, alas! virtue in this world is disowned and unrewarded."

"There you utter a great truth," said Rübezahl, "and it makes me very happy to have the honor of meeting at least one virtuous man. If agreeable to you, I wish you would come with me to my cell and there teach me your idea of virtue. I'm able to repay you for your trouble, for I have discovered the secret of making gold, and know how to prepare a liquid that will prolong life. Since you're so virtuous, you can certainly make best use of these two secrets which I shall impart to you in return for your kindness."

The stranger joyfully accepted the proposal. As he walked along, he spoke in the most glowing terms of his merits and of the sublime principles which he followed. He boasted that he had resisted all the temptations of the world, that gold was worthless in

---

[7] tippler, per original text

his estimation, and that he had never attempted to achieve glory in the sight of men.

Though Rübezahl listened attentively he made a very wry face. His silence encouraged the stranger to continue the details of his many virtues. Meanwhile, they'd reached the cell which, surrounded by a fine garden, was situated on the most beautiful spot on the mountains.

"You're hungry and most likely thirsty," said Rübezahl. "Rest here on this mossy bank in the shade while I prepare as good a meal as my poor cell will permit."

The stranger didn't need to be told twice. He stretched himself at full length and waited until his generous host brought a basket in which were fresh juicy fruits, fine white bread, and creamy cheese. In addition to these good things there were several bottles of homemade wine. The stranger set to with a will and enjoyed the meal heartily. His talkativeness was increased because he had quickly drunk one glass of wine after another. Presently his eyes became glazed and his tongue began to lisp, for altogether he had finished fully three bottles of wine.

"Aye! Aye!" said the hermit, putting the other bottles to one side, "you're in danger of violating the virtue of temperance." Thereupon our hero, with much solemnity, assumed a dignified air to conceal his condition from his host as much as possible.

Rübezahl now led him into a room where performed his chemical experiments.

There was a heap of small gold bars on a table, and the eyes of our hero rested covetously on the immense treasure. While the hermit absented himself for a moment the stranger put one of the bars into his pocket, and he would have taken others had not Rübezahl just then returned.

The hermit performed some chemical tricks and changed common red sand into grains of gold.

Following his host's directions our hero attempted the same, blew, shook, and rattled, but the sand remained sand. He grew frustrated and even muttered a curse because he was unsuccessful.

"Aye! Aye! my friend, patience does not seem to be one of your virtues. We shall now rest outside, and meanwhile you can teach me in what way I can follow your sublime example." The stranger started to follow Rübezahl, but the bar of gold became hundreds of pounds in weight, so that he was unable to move.

"What ails you now?" asked the hermit. Noticing plight of his guest, he said more sternly than before, "Respecting other people's property does not seem to be one of your virtues. You're in danger of committing a theft. Lay the gold bar on this pile."

Astonished and ashamed, the stranger emptied his pocket. His impudent boast of being a teacher of virtue had already failed the test on three different occasions. The hermit pretended to have forgotten what had happened, and showed himself still eager to know the foundation of his claim to virtue.

"Friend hermit," said the fellow in solemn tones, "the first thing to bear in mind is 'Shun temptation.' This is the safest course for mankind in general. For me — no temptation is too strong to resist. That I was tipsy a while ago was due to excessive thirst which no man can overcome. My failure to change sand into gold which you had done so easily will naturally explain my loss of temper and the matter of the gold bar was only a trick to learn just what kind of man you were."

"Oh! You miserable liar," cried Rübezahl in great wrath, "you can't even respect the truth. I'm at last tired of your bragging about virtue."

Thereupon a frightful storm arose. It whisked the braggart instantly far over the mountains to the good town of Hirschberg and into the middle of the market place, which was then full of people.

There he found himself rooted to the spot. Hanging from his neck over his breast was a sign with this inscription :

PUNISHMENT FOR INTEMPERANCE,
ILL TEMPER, THEFT AND LYING.

THE MOUNTAIN MEADOW

IN THE VILLAGE OF SCHREIBERHAU lived a poor man named Kilian. He had twelve healthy children for whom his limited means provided the barest support. His wife was so busy from early morning until late at night in household cares for this merry crowd that she found little time to help earn bread for the dozen hungry ones. They had a most hearty appetite, and at meal time opened wide their mouths like young swallows for whom the parent birds bring home a supply of food. The good father found his task a heavy one, for he was only a cottager with a small garden.

He had neither cow nor farm. He had but one goat. He was often at a loss to procure fodder for this poor animal, and yet the goat was indispensable. It supplied the youngest children with good nourishment, and there was sufficient milk besides to enable the good mother to furnish a tasty oatmeal porridge on Sundays.

Kilian's custom was to go up the mountain in summer to mow the rich grass, which he bundled and stored in a little shed on the spot. In winter, after the first snow had fallen, he drew it down in a rude homemade sled.

One morning the careworn man, his scythe on his shoulder, went as usual on his mountain trip. He was accompanied by the three oldest boys that they might help him rake the hay and store it in the shed. While they were busily at work, the perspiration running in big drops from their foreheads, a man on horseback rode by. It was like he sprang from the earth. When he reached Kilian and his children he stopped, turned around and snarled at the terrified father, "How dare you mow up here? Who gave you permission to do so?"

"Ah, noble sir," answered the poor man, "pardon me if I have trespassed on your land. I was ignorant that the grass was owned by anyone in particular. I always believed it belonged to anyone who took the trouble to carry it away. Still, if I have done wrong and have taken your property, don't judge me too harshly, but let mercy temper justice. Tell me where you live and I shall gladly bring it and store it in your barns."

The horseman allowed his large dark eyes to rest on the petitioner for a while, and then said, "You appear to me to be an honest man. This time you may go unpunished, but never again dare to claim a single blade of grass on this mountain."

"I thank you, noble sir, for your leniency. I shall take good care to obey your commands. For all there is in this world I wouldn't enrich myself with the goods of another. That I can no longer procure winter fodder for my goat is indeed a hard blow. Right here there was a rich growth of grass mixed with wholesome strength-giving herbs so that the animal thrived[8] and gave milk in plenty. Still I must seek other help in my need. See, noble sir, I'm poor in land and money and rich only in children: six boys and six girls for whom I must provide bread sit at my table. I have this burden daily and yet my heart rejoices when I see their red cheeks and laughing eyes. I couldn't spare a single one of them; they have all endeared themselves to my heart. If you're a father yourself, you can easily understand me."

"You're a tender father," answered the man, "and

---

[8] For the record, the proper term is throve. Or it was.

as the grass is so necessary to you and you have neither field nor farm, you may take away your winter supply of fodder as before. This piece of ground shall be yours and shall remain so. Go tomorrow in good time to the town clerk of Schreiberhau, and you will there find a deed of donation so that the land will be yours and your children's after you."

Who now was happier than Kilian? As he knew no other way of testifying his thanks he was overflowing in his expressions of gratitude. The lads made many bows, for their mother had taught them politeness. She had sometimes impressed her lessons with a hazel stick. This she considered a good aid and one that helped more than mere instruction. Father and children wished to kiss the hand of the noble gentleman, but he galloped away on his swift horse and in a moment was lost to sight.

Midday was long past when Kilian and his three children, in a happy frame of mind, went down the mountain. The poor man hurried to tell the news that he had become a landowner to his good wife. She looked at him incredulously and said, "Dear husband, the vicious Mountain Spirit has only been making a fool of you. You wouldn't be the first on whom he has played his pranks."

At these words Kilian felt as if cold water had been poured over him. In the first move of joy he had embraced his wife and had whirled her around the room like a top. He now let go, looked at her with sorrowful eyes and went out very sadly. He thought to himself, "We shall see tomorrow whether there will be a deed of gift for me at the town clerk's. If the stranger has had it legally drawn up and his name signed to it, the matter is settled and no one can dispute my rights."

Kilian awaited the next day with impatience. He passed the night uneasily and was tortured with most frightful dreams. He dreamed that his children were changed to goats and the house goat to a horned horse on whose back he flew through the air, while his wife clung tightly to the tail and made the journey with him. He awoke bathed in perspiration.

He was glad that it was only a dream that had tormented him. As soon as the sun shone brightly in his room he dressed quickly and rushed to the office of the town clerk.

He made known his business with much stuttering and stammering, for he had lost his confidence of the day before. Anxiously he awaited the answer. The official looked at him, shook his head, and thought, "Constant worry over the cares of life has taken away what little wit he ever had; he is not exactly right in his mind, and no wonder." No, the official had neither seen nor heard anything about the deed of gift. Kilian now bitterly lamented that he could no longer provide for the winter and that he would be obliged to sell the goat.

Suddenly a heavy gust of wind rattled the window, blew it open and drove in a roll of paper which fell on the floor. The clerk unfolded it, and saw that it was the deed of gift of which Kilian had spoken. It was stamped with the great official seal of the town of Hirschberg, and thus the legality of the document couldn't be questioned.

The happy man hurried home to inform his wife and children of the good news. All experienced the greatest joy, as a burden had been lifted, and in their hearts they thanked Rübezahl a thousand times. The poor cottager went daily to the mountain to mow the grass, for during the night it grew so luxuriantly that each succeeding morning the scythe cut it with difficulty.

When the time came, Kilian carried the hay down and stored it. There was a much greater quantity than he had expected, for when he supposed he had reached the last bundle, he always found more. It became necessary to enlarge his little shed as it was now entirely too small. The goat got along wonderfully, and anyone could see that magic was at work. She became larger and stronger and gave so much milk that there was always more than was needed.

The housewife said one day to her husband, "You remember that in my maiden days I served as stewardess in a castle, and that I had the keys of kitchen and cellar. At that time I learned to prepare goats' milk, to curdle it, to season it with caraways and salt, and to make it into cheese for the market. Let us see if we can't begin this business; there is nothing like trying."

Her husband rejoiced at the proposal and entered into the new plan with zeal. The goat supplied milk in abundance, and their cheese became celebrated far and near. It soon followed that Kilian and his wife, by industry and economy, began to live in comfort. They never forgot, however, their former poverty. They were charitable to their less fortunate neighbors and their sudden prosperity -- which they readily attributed to Rübezahl -- didn't provoke the usual envy or jealousy of others. Father and children went up the mountain every summer and mowed and cured the grass.

The piece of land donated by Rübezahl was inherited by Kilian's children and his children's children. The Kilians were a large family and their lands and farms were to be found in every quarter of Silesia.

THE MAGIC PEAS

"MASTER," SAID HEROLD, the industrious young journeyman, to his employer the cabinet maker, "though I would cheerfully stay longer with you, I must go, and I ask your permission to do so. My mother writes me that my father has been very ill for a long time. It is my duty to return home and work for my parents with these sound, strong arms."

"Since you have such a good reason I must let you go at once," answered the master, "but we shall all miss you, for I have never had a more industrious workman, nor a more skillful one. I would gladly raise your wages could you remain, but I see that it can't be. Return then in God's name to your home. You will be able to make a living wherever you go."

The young man strapped on his knapsack and took leave of his master. He did this sadly, for he had been treated like a son.

Herold could have saved a lot of money had it not been for his good heart. He had used the greater part of his earnings to help a companion who had been ill for a long time. The good Herold had now but little money to bring with him on his long journey home to Bohemia.

The master at parting slipped a bright dollar into his hand. The brave lad instead of keeping it brought it to his sick friend.

Herold, however, had a stout heart, and his confidence in God and in his fellow-men didn't desert him. On his road he often found a good lodging without paying for it. Indeed, many travelers on the way gave the merry singing lad a piece of money. He finally reached the Riesengebirge and was on the lookout for a resting place, when he saw a little hut on one of the loneliest spots on the mountain.

The owner, a strange, harsh-looking man, made a bed of fragrant hay and gave him a generous supper of bread and cheese. Next morning when Herold asked for the bill the host said gruffly, "Have you so much to spare? Keep it for your parents. They can make use of it. I don't mind a piece of bread and cheese."

"Very well," answered Herold, "I thank you for your kindness." He thought to himself, however, that if there had been more civility his obligation would have been greater. He was about to leave when the man placed a pot of peas on the table and said in his rough way, "If you want to eat something before you start, don't be so proud. There is a seat and here is a spoon."

But Herold thanked him and didn't wait for the meal. He could neither rest nor have peace until he reached home to see for himself how his sick father was getting along.

He took, however, a double handful of the peas lest he might give offense, and then went on his way. During the rest of his journey he didn't pass another house. He was glad to eat some of the dry peas, and he found them so tasty that he kept a goodly portion for his mother.

It was late in the evening when he reached his native village. As he went by the window where his mother had so often sat spinning, he forgot that he was weak from hunger and travel. How his heart beat as he opened the door! How quickly his weary feet brought him to the little room where poverty reigned as he had feared it would! His father lay groaning on a wretched bed and, although the weather was cold, no fire burned on the hearth. His mother showed marks of care and anxiety, and her eyes, weak from crying, didn't at first recognize her son.

As he greeted her and seized her hand she fell into his arms. She seemed as happy as if she had never had a sorrow or a care. The invalid father cried out joyfully and attempted to rise from his bed, but was unable to do so from weakness. "That is hunger," said he softly. "Since yesterday neither your mother nor myself has eaten a morsel."

Herold sought eagerly in his pocket for the peas in order that his father and mother might at least have a mouthful. He himself would immediately seek the head of the joiners' guild, he would offer to work for even very smallest wages if he could earn some money to relieve the immediate wants of his parents.

He laid the peas on the table and grasped his cap. Tired though he was, he would cheerfully work through the entire night that his parents might no longer go hungry. The mother lighted a pine knot that he might see his way down the outer steps. As she passed by the table some shining objects attracted her attention. Herold also noticed them. They were the peas which the gruff old man had given him. Mother and son soon convinced themselves that the peas had become pure gold.

Joy and happiness now reigned in the little poverty-stricken home. Herold had his hands full attending to everything. Soon there was a pot of savory soup ready for all three. He next sought a doctor for his sick father, who soon recovered. Herold now set himself up in business.

His skill, industry and fair dealing won him many customers and he was soon able to employ four apprentices. His business prospered and he was able to care for his parents to his heart's content.

In addition to his many other charities, and in thankful remembrance of his good fortune at the hands of Rübezahl, his gruff mountain host, he allowed no year to pass without distributing fifty bushels of peas among the village poor. Heartfelt blessings richly repaid him for his generous gift.

MOTHER ILSE

ONE DAY as Rübezahl was sunning himself by the hedge of his famous garden, a woman whose strange appearance attracted his attention came along. She had one child at the breast and one on her back. She led another by the hand while a larger boy carried a rake and an empty basket. She was about to gather a load of leaves for her goats.

"A mother," thought Rübezahl, "is truly a worthy creature. Here is one who trudges along with four children, attends to all their wants without murmuring, and will later burden herself further with a heavy load."

These thoughts put him in a good-natured mood and encouraged him have a conversation with the good woman. After having seated her children on the grass, the mother began to strip leaves from the bushes. The youngest child was bored and began to cry. The mother stopped her work, petted and fondled the child, took him up and danced around singing. Having soothed him to sleep, she returned to her work.

Then the gnats bothered the little sleeper so that he awoke and began to cry again. The patient mother ran into the woods and plucked wild strawberries, and finally placed the baby at her breast. These motherly actions pleased Rübezahl. The child who had been carried on the mother's back grew stubborn and wouldn't be quieted. He was a headstrong youngster who threw away the berries that his mother gave him and cried loudly with all his might. The mother finally lost patience and said, "Rübezahl! Come and eat up this cry-baby."

The Mountain Spirit immediately appeared in the usual form of a wood burner, approached the woman and said, "Here I am, what do you want?"

At this, the woman was terrified, but as she was brave and determined she mustered up courage and said, "I only called you to make my children keep still. As they are now quiet I don't need you. Thank you for your good wishes."

"Don't you know," said he, "that no one calls Rübezahl without receiving punishment? I'll keep you to your word. Give me the cry-baby and I'll eat him. I have not had so tender a morsel for a long time." He stretched out his sooty hand to seize the child.

A hen, when the hawk hovers high in air, first gathers her chickens to the safety of the henhouse with anxious clucking. Then with feathers pruned and wings outstretched, she begins an unequal fight with the enemy. So Ilse shook her sinewy fist at the very beard of the intruder and shouted, "Monster, you must tear the mother heart out of my breast before you can touch my child."

Rübezahl, who had not expected so determined an attack, shrank timidly back. In his interactions with mankind he had not experienced such stout resistance. He smiled pleasantly at the woman and said, "Don't be angry, I'm not a man-eater as you suppose and I shall do you and your children no harm. Let me have the little fellow; he pleases me and I'll bring him up like a nobleman; I'll clothe him in silk and velvet and make of him a trusty fellow who will later on support father and mother and brothers. I'll give you a hundred dollars for him."

"Ha!" laughed the mother. "So the youngster

pleases you? Yes, he is just an angel and is not for sale at any price."

"Fool!" answered Rübezahl. "Have you not three other children, all of whom are a trouble and an anxiety? You can support them only with difficulty, and you're burdened with them day and night."

"Very true! For that reason am I a mother, and I must do my duty by them. Children make sorrow but they also make joy."

"Great joy! Always a bother, leading them, washing for them, and putting up with their rudeness and squalling."

"Surely, Master, you little know a mother's joy! A single pleased look, the merry smiles and innocent prattle of the youngsters, sweetens every trouble and lightens every labor. See the little angel now! How he hangs on to me, the little flatterer! Now he's not the one who cried! Ah, would I had a hundred hands! They would lift you and carry you and work for you, you little darlings!"

"Your husband then has no hands to work for them?"

"Yes, he has. He uses them. Sometimes even I feel them."

"What! Your husband dares to lift his hands to you? To such a wife! I'll twist his neck, the scoundrel!"

"You will have steady employment if you twist the neck of every husband who raises his hand to his wife. Husbands are a troublesome lot; for the proverb goes, 'Married life, full of strife.' I must submit, otherwise why did I marry?"

"Well, was it not a foolish thing for you to marry, since you knew all this?"

"That may all be, but Steffen was a lively lad who earned good wages, and I was but a poor lass without a dowry. He asked me in marriage, was willing to take me as I was, and the bargain was made. Later on his generosity ceased, but I still have him."

"Perhaps you have changed him through your stubbornness."

"Oh ! He has driven that out of me already. Steffen is a miser. When I ask him for money he rages worse than you do sometimes here on the mountains. He reproaches my poverty, and I must keep silence. If I had only brought him a dowry, I would repay him for his faultfinding."

"What business does your husband follow?"

"He trades in glassware. He earns his living hard enough. Year in and year out, the poor fellow must carry his heavy loads over the mountains from Bohemia. If he breaks a glass on the way, myself and the poor children must pay for it. Still one must put up with such things."

"And you can love a man who treats you so?"

"Why not? Is he not the father of my children? Later they will repay us when they have grown up."

"Poor consolation! Children seldom repay the care and anxiety of their parents. They will take the last penny from you when the Kaiser drafts them into the army, and later on they will be killed by the enemy."

"Oh! It will not bother me if they are killed. They will die for their Kaiser and their Fatherland. That is only their duty. But they may also make their way in the world and take care of their old parents."

Rübezahl now repeated his offer about the boy, but Ilse didn't answer as she gathered the leaves into her basket and bound the crying little one once more firmly on her back. Rübezahl turned as if to go. As Ilse's burden was so heavy she found it difficult to stand erect. She called him back.

"I called for you once," she said, "but I didn't need you. I now kindly wish you to help me to put this load on my back, and if you feel like doing something further you can give a penny to buy sweets for the little lad who seemed to please you so much. The father returns home tomorrow and will bring us some white bread from Bohemia."

"I shall cheerfully help you," answered the Mountain Spirit; "but if I can't have the boy, I have no gift for him."

"Very well," answered Ilse; and she went on her way.

The farther she went the heavier became her load. She almost sank beneath its weight. She soon had to stop to catch her breath every few steps. This didn't seem right; she feared that Rübezahl had played one of his tricks on her and by his magic had put stones among the leaves. She set her basket on the first convenient ledge and examined it thoroughly, but she found nothing but leaves. She half emptied it, but she still found her load very heavy, and she once more had to lighten the basket. This surprised her, for she was very strong. She had often brought home the hamper piled high with leaves and never felt such fatigue.

On reaching home she attended to her household duties, threw the leaves to the goats and the kids, gave the children their supper, put them to bed, said her evening prayers and was quickly in a sound sleep.

The industrious wife was roused to her daily tasks, not only by the early dawn, but also by the wakeful baby who loudly cried and demanded his breakfast. As usual, she first went with her milk pail to the goat stall. What a shocking sight met her eyes! The faithful house friend, the old goat, lay stark and stiff, stone dead. The kids, however, still turned their eyes piteously, and stretched out their tongues. Severe convulsions showed that they were not far from death. The good wife had never as yet met with such a misfortune. Palsied with terror, she sank on a bundle of straw. She held her apron before her eyes, for she couldn't bear to witness the agony of the poor animals. She sighed deeply.

"Ah, wretched woman that I am! What shall I do?

What will my hard man say when he comes home? Ah! All God's blessings in this world have left me."

But her good heart immediately rebuked her. "Were the dearly cherished animals," she thought, "God's only blessings on earth? What then is Steffen and what are our children?"

She felt ashamed at her thoughtlessness. "Let all the wealth in the world go, I still have my husband and my four children; the good God will not forsake us. Even if I have an odd quarrel with Steffen, that's nothing but a trifle. I lose nothing by that. The harvest is at hand. I can go reaping, and in winter I'll spin until midnight. In this way I can get another goat; and when I have that, the children shall not want for milk."

With these thoughts she cheered up. She wiped away her tears When she raised her eyes she noticed that one of the leaves glittered like pure gold. She lifted it, examined it and found it as heavy as if it were indeed gold. She sprang to her feet, ran and joyfully showed it to her neighbor, the storekeeper's wife. This good woman at once recognized it as gold and gave her two dollars for it. All her grief was now forgotten.

The poor woman had never before had so much money at one time. She hastened to the baker's and bought bread and butter and cakes for the children. At the butcher's she got a leg of mutton for Stefan's dinner. She meant to have it ready for him when he reached home that night, tired and hungry from traveling.

How the children greeted their mother as she entered and gave them so unusual à breakfast!

She gave herself up to the motherly joy of feeding her hungry children. Her next task was to hide the animals that in her opinion had been bewitched by some evil spirit. She planned to hide the misfortune from her husband as long as possible. She didn't want to depress him with the bad news just after he had brought home his heavy load and had ended his long and toilsome journey.

Her astonishment passed all bounds as she looked by chance in the crib barn and saw it full of shining golden leaves. She concluded that the poor animals must have been killed by eating such indigestible food. She quickly sharpened the carving knife, opened the body of the old goat and found in her stomach a lump of gold as big as an apple. Similar lumps, though smaller, were in the stomachs of the three kids.

She had no idea what the extent of her wealth was. This began to weigh on her mind. She was restless and timid. She felt her heart beating wildly and didn't know whether she should hide the treasure in the closet or bury it in the cellar. She feared thieves and treasure hunters. She didn't want the miser Steffen to know. She had a well-founded fear that, tempted by greed, he would take it all and continue to keep her and her children in want. She thought for a long time how to manage matters, but came to no decision.

The village magistrate was a very kind man who comforted those in trouble, generously helped widows and orphans, and never tolerated injustice.[9] He would never spare the surly Steffen when that noisy house tyrant oppressed his good wife. Ilse went to this official, informed him fully of the adventure with Rübezahl, told how he had given her great riches and what her perplexities were. She proved the truth of her story by showing the treasure which she had brought with her.

The judge was astonished at the strangeness of the event. He rejoiced at the poor woman's good fortune, and thought deeply over some plan that would allow her to keep peaceable possession of her wealth without the interference of the greedy Steffen.

After some time he said, "Listen, my good woman. I have at last hit upon what I consider a good plan.

---

[9] It's elements like this that make this a fairy tale.

Have your gold weighed and let me keep it for you. I shall write a letter, in a foreign language to this effect: 'Your brother who emigrated years ago entered the Venetian service and afterward went to India where he died. In his will he left everything to you on condition that the judge of this village act as administrator, so that you and you only can profit by the inheritance. Personally I want neither reward nor thanks, but I must remind you that you owe something to Heaven for the blessing It has bestowed on you. I feel that you should remember the poor of the town, many of whom are in great distress."

Ilse, who was greatly pleased at this advice, cheerfully promised what he desired. The judge weighed the gold in her presence, put it in the office strong box and the good woman departed with a light and joyful heart.

Rübezahl had hated womankind ever since the fair Emma cheated him with the matter of counting turnips. On occasions, however, when he was well-disposed toward a needy woman he was generously ready with his help. The courageous Ilse had won his favor by her noble actions, but he was highly indignant at the tyrant Steffen. He earnestly wanted to punish him for his conduct to his faithful wife.

He decided to play him a vicious prank, one that would cause him pain, anxiety, and at the same time humble him so that he would feel indebted to his wife. Rübezahl wanted her, according to her own wish, to teach Stefan a lesson he wouldn't soon forget.

Rübezahl mounted the swift morning wind and swept over hill and valley, examining carefully, like a watchful spy, all the roads that led from Bohemia. When he saw a traveler with a load on his back he followed and investigated the nature of the burden. Luckily no wanderer carried glassware, otherwise he would have suffered injury without hope of remedy, even if he were not the man whom Rübezahl sought.

As a result, Steffen with his heavy load couldn't long escape the watchful eye of the Mountain Spirit. As evening was at hand, Rübezahl noticed a strong, lusty man with a large hamper on his back. The load he carried rattled under his firm step. Rübezahl rejoiced as he saw him in the distance and at last felt sure of his prey. He prepared to carry out his plan.

The panting Steffen had almost reached the mountain top and had but one more height to climb. Then it would be down hill all the way to his home. He walked faster, for the hill was steep and his load heavy. He often had to stop and rest. From time to time he put his knotty stick under the hamper to lessen the pressing weight on his back. He wiped away the perspiration from his forehead. With the last efforts of his almost exhausted strength, he reached the summit and a straight even path lay before him to the opposite slope.

Midway in the road was the cut-off stump of a pine tree whose trunk lay nearby. The top was level as a table. All around was long luxuriant grass. The prospect of such a comfortable resting place was so pleasing to the weary traveler that he put his heavy hamper on the stump and lay down in the soft grass in the shade.

While resting he considered what profit his goods would bring. After careful calculation, he decided that if he spent nothing for his home and let his industrious wife worry about providing food and clothing, he would have enough to buy and load a donkey at the Schmiedeberg Fair. The thought of the donkey carrying his load while he trudged comfortably alongside was stimulating at a time when his shoulders were still aching from his burden. His thoughts wandered farther in his daydreams.

"Once I have the donkey, I shall soon have a horse; and once I have a horse in the stable, I must have a field to raise oats for him. My acre will soon become two, then four, in time a small farm and finally a large one, and then, then— I shall buy Ilse a new dress."

He got that far in his castle building when Rübezahl suddenly let loose a whirlwind which overturned the hamper and broke its fragile contents into a thousand pieces. This came as a thunderclap to Steffen. At the same time he heard a mocking laugh in the distance. He considered everything malicious, and, as the violent and unexpected wind seemed unnatural and both stump and tree trunk had vanished, he was not long in guessing the mischief-maker.

"Oh!" moaned he, "Rübezahl, you source of all my misfortune, what harm have I ever done to you that you should deprive me of the bread I have so honestly earned. Alas! I'm undone for life."

Hereupon, he fell into a sort of frenzy and shouted out all imaginable abuse against the Mountain Spirit in order to excite him to wrath.

"Come, scoundrel," he cried, "come and throttle me, since you have deprived me of everything I had in the world."

Life at that moment as worthless as his broken glassware. Rübezahl was neither seen nor heard again. The impoverished Steffen decided that unless he wished to carry the basket home empty he must gather up the fragments. These at least he could exchange at the glass factory for a few water glasses as a new start in business.

Sunk in thought like a ship-owner whose vessel with man and mouse has been engulfed by the angry ocean, he went down the mountain side. Though his brain was occupied with a thousand sorrowful thoughts, he was also scheming how to repair the damage and set his business on foot again.

He remembered his wife's goats. He knew she loved them almost as if they were her own children, and he knew that she would never willingly give them up. He hit upon the following plan. He would mention nothing of his loss at home; neither would he return by day, but would creep in about midnight, drive the goats to Schmiedeberg and with the money from their sale, purchase a new stock. He also decided as part of his plan to be argumentative, and to act harshly as if the animals had been stolen in his absence through his wife's carelessness.

With this intention the unhappy glass peddler crept near the village and anxiously waited for midnight that he might steal his own goats. At the stroke of twelve he started on his thieving expedition, climbed the low fence and crept with beating heart to the goat stalls. He was both afraid and ashamed to be caught by his wife in so wicked an action.

Contrary to custom, he found the stable unlocked. This surprised but at the same time pleased him. This carelessness would furnish a reason for carrying out his plans. Everything in the stable was desolate and dreary, nothing with life was there, neither goats nor kids. In his first fright he fancied that some other thief had been before him, one more successful than he.

Misfortunes, he thought, never come singly. Doubly grieved, now that his last attempt to build up his business was a failure, he sank on the straw and gave himself up to gloomy thoughts.

After Ilse's return from the magistrate's office, she was busy preparing a good meal for her husband. The judge had accepted an invitation to be in attendance. He promised to bring a bottle of wine to make a merry feast at which he could inform Steffen of his wife's inheritance, and the conditions under which he could have share and part in the same.

Toward evening Ilse looked anxiously for Steffen, who as far as she knew never came home. At last she hurried impatiently toward the village, looked with her bright black eyes along the highroad and at last became uneasy at the delay. When night fell she returned to her little room, worried and filled with foreboding and without thinking of supper. For a long time no sleep visited her tear-filled eyes, but toward morning she fell into a heavy, restless slumber.

Anxiety and vexation were Steffen's companions as he sat in the goat stable. He was so cast down that he hardly trusted himself to rise and knock at the door of his humble home. At last he mustered up courage and knocked once or twice and called in a sad voice, "Open, dear wife ; it is I, your husband."

As soon as Ilse heard his voice she ran to the door and embraced him joyfully. He met her endearments coldly, put down his hamper, and threw himself on a chair. When the cheerful wife saw his misery, it touched her heart.

"What's the matter, dear husband?" said she in a tone full of sympathy. "What ails you?"

His only answer was sighs and groans. Again she asked him the cause of his sorrow. Stefan's heart was so full he could no longer conceal his misfortune from his trusting wife. As she realized the trick played by Rübezahl, she readily guessed the well-meant design of the Mountain Spirit and couldn't refrain from laughing.

This was something that Steffen wouldn't have tolerated had he been in a more settled frame of mind. This time he didn't criticize her mirth, but inquired anxiously after the goats. Ilse knew then that the house tyrant had been spying everywhere.

"Of what concern to you are my goats?" she said. "As yet you have not asked about the children; the goats are outside in the pasture. Don't let Rübezahl's prank disturb you, don't you bother about it. Who knows but that he or someone else will console us for our loss?"

"You can wait long for your consolation," said Steffen.

"I don't know about that," said Ilse. "What's unexpected often happens. Don't be cast down, Steffen. Even if you have no glassware and I have no goats, we not only have four healthy children, but we have four strong arms to work for them and ourselves."

"Ah! God pity us!" cried the unfortunate man. "If the goats are gone, you can drown the children. I can't feed them."

"Well," answered Ilse, "I can."

At this point the friendly judge entered. Outside the door he had overheard the conversation.

He now had his say and he berated Steffen, lecturing him soundly that greed is the root of all evil. After he had reproved him sufficiently, the judge announced the news of Ilse's rich inheritance. He drew from his pocket the foreign letter that appointed him, the village judge, executor of the will. He announced that the wealth of the deceased brother-in-law was already in secure hands.

Steffen was astounded and could do nothing but nod his head dumbly when, at the mention of the Republic of Venice, the judge respectfully touched his hat. After Steffen recovered some of his senses, he embraced his wife affectionately and assured her of his true love.

From this time on Steffen was the friendliest and most amiable of husbands, a loving father to his children, and a thrifty and industrious manager, for idleness was not one of his faults. The judge from time to time changed the gold to current coin, and bought a large farm which Steffen and Ilse managed for the remainder of their lives. He put the surplus out at interest and carefully and honestly managed the capital entrusted to him. Personally he received no reward and he gladly distributed the money given to him by Ilse among the poor.

In her old age the faithful mother experienced the greatest joy in her children. They proved themselves worthy of her noble struggles. They always retained the sincerest affection for her, and treated with the greatest respect and veneration the mother who had labored so earnestly for them. Rübezahl's favorite became a brave soldier and served for a long time in the Thirty Years' War under Wallenstein in the Kaiser's army.

C. F. ARCIERI

THE JOURNEYMAN

JOSEPH, the son of poor parents in Schmiedeberg, had wandered through Germany, as was customary for journeymen at that time. He desired to perfect himself in his trade and where possible to earn something with which to help his parents. He was returning home over the Riesengebirge, and, as he looked down from the summit and saw his native village far below bathed in sunshine, his heart was sad and sorrowful.

He was returning home as poor as when he had started out.

"What a joy it would have been for me," he mused gloomily as he leaned on his staff, "if I could have brought home a purse full of bright dollars and emptied it into the hands of my dear parents. Alas! I can't even bring home a Sunday dress for my mother, or a pipe and tobacco for my father, or even a silk neckerchief. Unfortunately in Vienna I was sick for five months and could earn nothing. All my savings melted away. Ah! I'm a downright unfortunate fellow."

"My friend," suddenly spoke someone near him, "does your road go by yonder lake and, if so, would you be willing to do me a favor?"

Joseph looked wonderingly about him and saw an aged monk who, despite his weak and feeble appearance, carried a heavy stone on his back.

The young man removed his cap and said cordially, "Indeed, reverend father, my way lies in that very direction and I'm quite ready to help you in any way possible."

"Take this stone, then, and bring it to the lake. I have made a vow to remove one of the stones of my cell each day and throw it into the lake. Today, however, I'm prevented by illness. Do this for me and I know that you will not regret your kindness. And since, perhaps, the wicked fiend may tempt you, I wish strongly to impress on you that it will render me very unhappy if you don't scrupulously keep your word."

"Have no anxiety on that point," replied Joseph, "I shall carry the stone and throw it into the lake no matter what happens."

He took the heavy load, bowed cordially to the monk, and set out on his errand. When he arrived at the lake, he saw sitting on the opposite shore a well-dressed man who appeared to be reading a book very attentively. As Joseph was about to cast the stone into the water, what was his astonishment to find that it had changed to pure gold!

"Now my parents' poverty is at an end," he shouted joyfully. "With all this gold I can buy them the finest house in the village and besides I can set myself up in business. But," he added suddenly, "didn't the monk tell me that I would make him unhappy if I didn't keep my word? This is perhaps a temptation of the evil one to make me break my promise and thus cause misfortune to the good monk. Then again, may it not have been his intention to test my common sense; for who, in his right mind, would throw away such an enormous treasure with which so much good could be done?"

He turned about quickly, intending to pursue his way homeward and to keep the gold. But there was a still, small voice within him that wouldn't be silent. The words of the monk recurred to him: "You will render me unhappy if you don't keep your promise.”

His good spirit conquered. He stepped quickly to the edge of the lake and threw the lump of gold into the water. How great was his astonishment as he watched the gold float like a cork to the opposite shore, where it was taken out without any trouble by the well-dressed stranger!

“How unfortunate I am!” sighed the poor fellow as he noticed this. “A few dollars would help me out of all my trouble, and yonder stranger, who is apparently well-to-do, takes the treasure I was compelled to throw away.”

Sadly he started on his way home. He was sunk so deeply in thought that he wandered from the road and found himself in the woods. Realizing this he stepped onward quickly, for the sun had set, and he must rush to reach home, as he could ill afford to pay for a lodging even in the meanest hut.

His attention was attracted by a mournful groaning which appeared to come from the woods. Though he had but little time to spare, he felt he couldn't go on until he had seen whether any one was in need of help. Cautiously he approached the spot from which the groans came, and there he found, lying on the ground, a donkey that had fallen under a load of wood.

He at once relieved the poor animal and helped him to his feet. The donkey immediately started on what seemed to be a beaten path and Joseph decided to follow him, hoping in this way to reach a human habitation. When the darkness became so dense that he could no longer see his gray companion plainly enough to follow him, he mounted the donkey. He had hardly done this when the latter started off at a rapid pace and didn't halt until he had reached a ruined hut. There the donkey peacefully stretched himself on a heap of moss and dry leaves under a roof which was almost entirely open to the elements. Joseph considered it best to do the same, and he was soon asleep, overcome with fatigue and weariness.

When he awoke next morning, the donkey had disappeared and he found himself alone. He saw also to his dismay that someone had emptied his knapsack of his few articles of clothing and linen, all he possessed in the world.

This was a new misfortune for poor Joseph, and he wept bitterly. "How my good parents will be shocked when I return empty-handed, almost a beggar. But I shall keep this last sorrow from them as long as I can, until I prepare them gradually for it." So spoke Joseph as he filled his knapsack with leaves and moss.

When, at length, he reached the little house where his parents lived, he was surprised to see the stranger who had found the lump of gold passing by. Joseph looked after him sadly and thought how comfortable and stately he appeared, and how on the other hand poverty itself was stamped on the little home with its broken windows mended with paper.

The long-looked-for son was joyfully welcomed by his parents, and his mother took his knapsack from his back. "Aye! Aye!" she laughed, "how heavy it is! Our good Joseph must have had luck on his travels."

The good mother fancied, as she said, that Joseph had indeed had good luck; but the latter knowing all the circumstances as they really were was almost broken-hearted at her joyous reception. In spite of his reluctance to give her pain he was unable to respond to her welcome and looked at her despairingly.

The unhappy youth was about to confess when, noticing the monk pass by the window, he ran out quickly. But the monk was nowhere to be seen, and Joseph returned sadly into the house. His mother had opened the knapsack and was emptying it. To his astonishment Joseph saw her taking out the suit of clothes worn by the rich stranger. He was not a little puzzled to explain how it had got into his knapsack, but his astonishment was still greater as his mother next took out a large stone which shone in the sunlight like pure gold. On it were carved the words, "To the faithful youth from an unknown friend."

Joseph cried out in a loud voice, "Rübezahl! Rübezahl!" and folded his hands in a devout prayer in which the happy parents joined.

THE WONDER STAFF

A YOUNG APOTHECARY living in Schmiedeberg, whose daily occupation was to prepare salves and make all kinds of pills, found his chief pleasure in collecting rare plants and in pressing and arranging them neatly in his portfolio. On his free days he wandered over the mountains and through the valleys; and he even sought the gloomy clefts and ravines of the Riesengebirge for the velvety moss which here and there clung to the damp moist rocks.

One day he had filled his specimen box with these tender products of the plant world, and with quick steps was hurrying homeward. He suddenly realized, coming from a near-by thicket, the bent form of an old man whose weak, decrepit shoulders were burdened beneath the weight of a large pile of dry bundled twigs.

"Old father," said the young man in a friendly tone, "how can you load your weak back with such a burden? Is there no one to carry your wood for you?"

"I have neither wife nor child," answered the man, "and I must gather my winter fuel myself. It would be vain for me to seek anyone who would carry it to my hut without payment."

"I'll gladly carry it," said the apothecary, lifting the bundle in his strong arms and following the old man, who looked gratefully at him. The stranger had a peculiar expression. A look of cleverness shone from out his dark eyes. His curved nose reminded one of an eagle's beak, and around his mouth were lines indicative of merriment and goodness of heart. The long snow-white beard that reached to his waist was his most noticeable feature.

"I fear you will regret your kindness," said the old man after a pause, "for I live a good step from here. Remain with me tonight, and in the morning you can admire the sunrise in the mountains. It is indeed a beautiful sight. Whoever has seen it will never forget it, were he even to enjoy the same sight every day. You will then not regret having brought home my load."

"Who told you that I would regret it?" was the ready answer. "If I were able to help anyone and failed to do so, that indeed would be something I should regret. But I can't stay with you to-night. You see I'm an apothecary, and every day I must mix drugs and spread plasters. What would the sick people of Schmiedeberg do tomorrow if Andreas Liebekind were not at his post to attend to their wants? If I were not so poor, I would travel through the wide world. My first trip would be to the Alps, where there are noble herbs, roses, violets, gentian, and edelweiss in the greatest abundance. I would fill my box and bring home the rarest specimens. I have no money, however, for traveling and I'm little likely to have it during my lifetime, for a poor apothecary does not amass riches."

Chatting like this they arrived at the stranger's hut, where Andreas set down his load and with a friendly handshake bade farewell. The old man quickly opened the bundle, took a thick stick and gave it to the apothecary with these words, "Take this. It will be a support to you on your journey down the mountain."

Not wishing to offend the old man, Andreas accepted the stick, although he couldn't conceive what use he could make of it. When he had gone some distance he turned and cordially waved his hat. In a very little while he realized that he had strayed from the path.

"Ah!" he sighed, "this makes it two miles farther to go. In the meanwhile it will be pitch dark and my master will rate me soundly for returning so late. I wish I were at the Schmiedeberg town hall with the drug store close at hand, for I would then be at home."

Suddenly he stood in the market square in front of the store. His master was leaning against the open door of his shop, comfortably smoking his pipe. Andreas, all embarrassed, gazed at the houses about him. Finally he went toward the shop to convince himself that it was really his master whom he saw. In this strange way, he had reached home without any exertion whatever on his part.

Shaking his head he went to his room and looked almost fearfully at the mysterious stick. He saw readily that magic had been at work, and that Rübezahl, in the form of a wood gatherer, had met him and had rewarded his kindness with the wonder-staff.

Now, with the swiftness of thought and at any time he chose, he could reach the most distant lands. Did he wish a sea bath, he only needed to turn Rübezahl's stick and the next moment he was on the island of Heligoland. After he had bathed in the salty flood, he needed only to whisper,

> " O'er hill and o'er valley,
> come, quick set me down
> At my home in the
> far distant Schmiedeberg town."

After the last words he would find himself in his room, and a moment later he would be in the laboratory preparing mixtures that had, in the meanwhile, been slowly boiling over the coal fire.

His off days were veritable feast days for Andreas.

He would then wander, sometimes to the north, sometimes to the south. On one occasion he stood ready for travel, the mysterious stick in his hand. Turning the same, he murmured,

> "My tried, trusty staff, do your work : I
> would go To the land of the far distant
> Eskimo[10]."

He immediately found himself in a dimly lighted hut, partly dug out of the earth. Strings of fish hung over the hearth and the odor of train oil filled his nostrils. At a table-like mound of earth squatted the members of an Eskimo family, eating their meal of fish. They gazed wonderingly at the stranger who, unnoticed and quietly as a snowflake, had entered their dwelling.

They greeted him after their fashion, and furnished him with such eating and drinking as the hut afforded. By signs and gestures they gave him to understand that they were about to take a sleigh ride. They invited him to join them. He nodded assent and soon they all mounted a simple sled drawn by ten lusty dogs. The little vehicle flew like an arrow over the vast snow plain, and so jolly was the trip that Andreas, were it not that his nose froze so badly, would cheerfully have glided thus all the way back to Schmiedeberg.

After warming themselves on their return to the hut, all started on a bear hunt. This was a wonderful sight for the stranger. He forgot the cold as he saw the shaggy animals fiercely attack their foes. He admired the skill with which the Eskimos with their rude weapons conquered such formidable opponents. Glorious northern lights shone in the heavens, and Andreas would gladly have enjoyed a longer stay; but his watch showed him five minutes to six and at the last stroke of the hour he was due at his post. He

---

[10] Eskimo refers to more than one tribe living in Alaska

turned his staff and whispered,

> "To the Schmiedeberg drug store,
> come carry me fast,
> Or my time set for duty
> will surely be past."

The next moment he was home and in time to eat supper with the family.

He betrayed the secret of his magic staff to no one. He made his extensive travels without anyone being the wiser. The less he spoke, the more he wrote in his diary. Later he published a narrative of his travels, and earned so much that he was able to give up his position as apothecary's clerk.

Thereafter he traveled as a naturalist to every quarter of the known world. He visited all the countries of Europe, ascended the highest peaks of the snow-covered Alps, a feat accomplished by no one up to that time. He repeatedly witnessed the eruption of Etna and Vesuvius. He sojourned for months among the native tribes of Africa, in the primeval forests of America, in India, in China, in Japan and in Australia.

His journeys often led him to parts of the world now densely populated but little known at that time. He witnessed with delight the Amazon and its mighty tributaries, and rambled with pleasure among the ruined and desolate cities of once powerful empires. If a place didn't please him, or if he incurred danger from robbers or wild beasts, he needed only to turn his stick and he was saved.

After much wandering, and when advanced in years, he returned to his native town. He now, for the first time, told the people of his meeting with Rübezahl, and how nobly the latter had repaid him for his assistance. He was never separated from his staff. By day it stood by his armchair, and at night it found a place in his bed.

One morning the old man was found dead. His friends sought in vain for Rübezahl's magic staff. It had disappeared, and forever. Since then no man has been able to boast of having made so many, such extended, and at the same time such inexpensive journeys as the renowned naturalist of Schmiedeberg, Andreas Liebekind.

THE MANDRAKE

ON THE RIESENGEBIRGE there used to be the most beautiful pleasure garden in which the finest and rarest flowers in the world bloomed. It is sad that ordinary mortals never saw this garden, for the owner and lord was no other than Rübezahl, the Mountain Spirit, and he permitted entrance only to certain favored ones at special times and under peculiar conditions.

So, at least, was the legend among the good people of Silesia. It was believed also that there bloomed in this pleasure garden that most precious of all flowers, the mandrake[11]. Whoever plucked it on Saint John's night would be rich and happy for the rest of his life. But woe to the one who made the attempt unless he were pious, upright, and an orphan. Rübezahl, without mercy or pity, would break the neck of anyone else who dared to approach his garden.

This tradition was well known to a little fellow named Joseph who, with his sister, lived with a tender-hearted brewer, a distant relative. Both parents were long since dead. The little boy thought to himself, "When Saint John's day comes I shall try my luck. If I succeed, all will be well with myself and my sister. My adoptive father will also be benefited."

[11] Original text: Glücksmannlein. Glücksmannlein is one old German word for mandrake, also called "The Old Wise One."

On Saint John's day, therefore, Joseph started for the garden without saying a word to anyone about his plans. He put a piece of bread in his pocket in case he should be hungry, and he relied on the wayside springs to quench his thirst. He stepped out bravely in the direction of the mountains through the paths he had so often heard described.

On the mountain side he came to an inn. The innkeeper, who happened to be at the door, asked him in a friendly tone where he was going so late. "To pluck the mandrake. This is Saint John's day," was Joseph's answer.

The landlord shook his head and the lad went on his way. After he had gone a little distance he noticed a man walking quickly after him, a man whom he had seen at the inn door talking to the innkeeper when he spoke about going to Rübezahl's pleasure garden.

The boy knew him. He was a rich innkeeper from Breslau, who, the evening before, had been at the house of Joseph's adoptive father, the brewer. He and some of his friends had passed the night drinking and playing cards.

"Listen, Joseph," said he, "I'm going your way; let us travel together."

Joseph looked up in surprise, and thought, "Is he, too, going to try his luck? He looks healthy; I know he is rich; what more does he want?" He said nothing, however, and they went on together.

It was now growing late. The sun was sinking in the west and the cattle were going slowly homeward. The sounds of the evening bells came up the mountain from the little village in the valley below. Joseph, as was his custom, joined hands and devoutly said his evening prayers. The stranger laughed ; he had neither thought nor time for praying; he dreamed only of the mandrake and of all the wealth he would gain through its aid.

They soon reached Rübezahl's garden. They saw

the coveted flower growing in abundance, and it's beautiful bloom shone clear and silvery in the moonlight. Joseph's companion set to work greedily, plucked big handfuls, and stuck them into his pocket.

Suddenly an old man with a silver-white beard stood before them and in a voice like thunder shouted, "Halt!" Shocked and trembling in every limb the innkeeper shrank back, while the boy confidently approached the old man, offered him his hand and expressed his modest desire to have two flowers only.

"Child," said the old man in a friendly tone, "what will you do with them and why do you want just two?"

Joseph answered, "I want myself and my sister to be rich and happy. We should then be no longer a burden to our guardian, and we could repay him for all his kindness to us."

"You're a brave lad," said the old man, patting him gently on the head and giving him a large handful of The mandrake. He also stuffed the boy's pockets with the flowers, warning him to take good care of them and not to lose any. The boy thanked him politely.

The old man now turned to the innkeeper and thundered, "Who are you?"

"A poor man," was the answer, "who through no fault of his own has fallen into want, and who has also come to gather the mandrake in order to become rich and happy."

"Miserable creature! Out of my sight! Shall I make you rich just to enable you to gamble and squander? You're mistaken; the luck that I give here is meant only for the innocent and the orphan."

"Oh, master," said the trembling innkeeper, "I too am an orphan. My parents died while I was still a lad. I never knew them, and I was brought up by strangers."

Hardly had he said this when the old man grasped him by the throat and flung him down the steep mountain side. The boy sank to the earth in fright. He didn't dare to look up, and with beating heart he prayed devoutly to God. Then the old man took him by the hand and spoke to him softly and kindly and led him from the garden.

Meanwhile the brewer as well as the little sister were very worried about Joseph. You can judge therefore how great was their joy when he returned safely, bringing his pockets stuffed full of the coveted mandrake.

He generously divided the gift of the Mountain Spirit into three equal portions. All were astonished next morning to find that every leaf had changed into pure gold. All three were now rich, and what was better, happy as well, for the remainder of their lives.

THE MASTER OF HORSE

LATE ONE EVENING, a stately, aristocratic looking horseman knocked at the door of a solitary Silesian farmhouse. Three trumpeters and twenty coupled horses followed in a long train. All were tired and covered with dust, for they'd traveled a long distance and the day had been hot. Farmer Kurz opened the heavy courtyard gate and cheerfully greeted the stranger.

"I'm the master of horse from Biedenfeld, and I'm anxious to know if you can furnish me, my men and my horses with lodgings for the night. I'll won't be very inconvenient, for I carry my own supplies. Today I bought horses for our regiment, and as night has overtaken me, I shall not be able to reach the next village, which is still a great way off. You will do me a great favor by giving us shelter. You evidently have plenty of room."

"You're perfectly welcome to my humble accommodations if they suit you. Whatever I have is at your disposal. My wife will gladly prepare you a supper and a morning meal."

"I thank you for your kindness," said the officer, "but I carry my own provisions. I simply wish your man to give my horses a feed of hay, for which I shall pay well."

As he said this, he dismounted, and the trumpeters, unslinging their instruments which were hung over their shoulders by a heavy gilt cord, blew a melodious call like the sweet tones of silver bells. The horses pointed their ears, and in a gentle trot went, of their own accord, across the courtyard to the stables.

The housewife had meanwhile come to the open door and welcomed the guests with a hearty, "God greet you." She immediately began to bustle about, but the officer explained that nothing was desired but lodging. Every-thing else would be attended to by his trumpeters. These followed him to the upper story, where the farmer opened their parlor for the leader's use. They never opened the parlor except on such rare occasions as a christening, or some family festival. The trumpeters found comfortable accommodation in an adjoining room.

The master of horse was well content with the arrangements, and expressed his intention of taking a short rest before eating.

The farmer and his wife soon heard the opening and shutting of doors in the upper story. Frau Grete, full of curiosity, ascended a few steps to learn what was going on. She saw the trumpeters passing to and from their own room to that of the master, carrying the choicest dainties on silver plates. At this sight the good wife's mouth watered. She had never before smelled such appetizing odors as now filled the entire house.

She stepped softly down and told her husband of all the good things the master was enjoying upstairs. In a little while, footsteps were heard, and one of the trumpeters appeared with a large silver bowl which he set on the table with these words, "The master presents his compliments, and sends something from his table hoping that you will enjoy it."

It was a delicious soup, such as the astonished couple had never tasted before. When they'd finished, a second trumpeter brought a plate of delicious cauliflower and tender, juicy spare ribs, while a third trumpeter placed a bottle of costly Hungarian wine and two golden goblets on the table. They then brought brook trout and delicious venison, with dressing and salad. For dessert they had pudding and sweet confections, large, luscious grapes, lovely apples, mellow pears, and golden oranges. The farmer and his wife thoroughly enjoyed everything.

"Since our wedding day," said Kurz to his wife, "we have not had such a glorious feast. It is extremely kind of the noble gentleman to have remembered us so graciously. Let us then be merry, for such good fortune rarely comes to one's house."

Suddenly the trumpets were heard in the peaceful, stilly night and the soft mellow tones were reechoed again and again by the neighboring mountains. The happy pair listened and gave each other a puzzled look. As if by common consent they crept timidly to bed. Like frightened children they covered themselves, head and all, with the bedclothes, that they might neither see nor hear anything else.

Next morning they arose and hastened to the farmyard to attend to their daily occupations. They found their strange guests ready for their journey. All were mounted, and the horses were ranged in couples waiting for the accustomed trumpet signal.

The officer extended his hand and graciously thanked his host and hostess for the comfortable shelter he had found under their roof. He asked how much he owed, but the farmer wouldn't listen to such talk.

"Worthy sir," said he, twisting his cap respectfully, "you have repaid us abundantly. You have given me and my wife a meal such as we had never dreamed of, much less eaten. Should you ever pass this way again, stay with us. Everything we have is at your service."

"You have a good heart," answered the master, "but as I had an idea that you wouldn't accept payment, I have had something made ready for your breakfast. It is a dish with whose preparation your good wife is as yet unacquainted. In the crib your stable man will find payment for what the horses have eaten." The party then set off at a good round trot in the sunny morning. The trumpets again sounded. At this signal the horses broke into a gallop, and in a few moments all had disappeared.

The fanner clasped his wife by the hand and said, "That was undoubtedly the Lord of the Mountain. Come let us see what kind of breakfast he has served us as a farewell."

They entered the room and saw on the table a covered bowl. With fear and trembling they lifted the cloth, and a glittering spectacle greeted them. The bowl was filled to heaping with bright golden ducats. Then came rejoicing. The worthy Kurz danced merrily around the room, threw his cap to the ceiling, and shouted with all his might, "Hurrah! Hurrah!" Meanwhile Toffel, the stable man, brought in a handful of golden oats he had found in the crib.

Both were thus rewarded—the farmer and his man. Kurz bought a larger farm, and Toffel got the smaller one which his master had owned up to that time.

BEAUTIFUL SUSAN

MANY YEARS AGO there lived in the village of Lomnitz an aged couple; the charcoal burner, Stephen, and his devoted wife, Elsa. Hard work and many cares had early whitened the hair of both. Stephen had been helpless for some years with a most painful attack of gout, and he could earn nothing. As Elsa was obliged to attend her helpless husband day and night, little time was left her in which to procure the necessaries of life.

One fine summer day Stephen, leaning on his crutches, limped wearily out and sat on the bench before his door, so that God's dear sun might shine warmly on his poor, stiffened limbs. He looked wistfully at the distant woods in which formerly he had worked so industriously, and where he had earned his daily bread so happily and contentedly. Elsa joined him with her old-fashioned spindle, for at that time there were no spinning wheels in that section of the country. She sat beside the invalid and industriously turned the spindle. With an affectionate look she regarded the sick man whose distorted limbs indicated the great suffering he was so patiently enduring.

"Husband," she said, "don't look so sad. Who knows but that help is nigh? Don't give up all hope. Let us continue to put our trust in God. That has ever been our morning and evening prayer, and it has always brought us comfort. The man himself, who put those words in a hymn, lived in the greatest bodily agony but was finally delivered from it. So our pastor lately told us, and I listened devoutly to his consoling words. Perhaps, too, our trouble will soon end, and we shall be delivered from all care and you may work again as cheerfully as before."

"You're a good wife," said the old man. "You have ever had a ready and a comforting smile and a pious word. If I could only go to Warmbrunn. The bath cure has healed thousands; but that would take money, much money."

As the much tried pair chatted, they were interrupted by the appearance of a young and beautiful girl who came from the direction of the high road. She had a bundle under her arm, and she exhibited every appearance of great fatigue. She approached the cottage with the customary "God greet you," and in an accent strange to that neighborhood asked, "Will you kindly tell me if Stephen, the charcoal burner, lives in this village?"

"I'm the man you ask for," said the invalid; and the next moment the young girl was sobbing on his neck. "Then you're my dear uncle! I bring you the last words of my widowed mother, your dear sister; she was buried at Pentecost[12]."

"You're heartily welcome, my dear child," said the man kindly. "If you're willing to share our poverty, you have found a new home." Elsa now pressed the girl's hand affectionately, gently put back her flowing blond hair and gave her a hearty welcome.

"Be my new mother, Aunt Elsa," begged the maiden with soft voice. "I shall love you and care for you as if I were your own child."

After the exhausted maiden had been refreshed with a frugal meal of black bread and milk, Susan, for that was her name, told of the illness and death of her

---

[12] holy Pfingst Day, per original text

mother. She spoke of her own trials and how she had been obliged by hardhearted people to leave her clothes and little belongings for past due rent. Now that she had found her uncle she felt cheerful as to the future. Elsa prepared a bed of straw on which the exhausted maiden rested peacefully, and for the first time since her mother's death, her sleep was visited by pleasant dreams.

Although the care for daily bread had increased with Susan's arrival, a new life seemed to have entered the little home with the cheerful maiden. In a sweet, silvery voice she sang her little songs and accompanied herself on the zither. She prepared healing salves with which she carefully rubbed her uncle's stiff joints, and she always knew just what to say. Her kindly care always brought a gentle smile to the invalid's face.

The good Elsa, however, was quiet and sad; for her former apprehension was now doubled. If her scant means had allowed, she would most gladly have provided the poor orphan with suitable clothing and a comfortable bed. With concern she dreaded to the cold winter when both would be lacking. Both day and night she pondered deeply over the matter of providing for the girl, but she found no way out of her trouble.

One morning she was in the neighboring wood gathering fuel for winter use, for she was accustomed to provide whatever was necessary in good time. She heard near her a manly voice singing a merry song. She stopped working and looked at the singer. A man approached her from the forest and asked if she didn't need some of his wares. He was a herb collector. He dealt in wonderful salves and plants that healed all kinds of infirmities.

"Ah!" answered Elsa, "you hardly have the herb I want. My poor husband has been afflicted with gout for ten years. Could you relieve him in any way, I would give you with joy the only treasure I have, a silver medal presented to me on my confirmation day by my godfather."

The stranger said laughingly, "I may be able to help your husband without it being necessary for you to give up your medal. Gather your wood and lead me to your husband."

Susan had meanwhile made up the sick man's bed, swept the room and placed bread and milk, the usual breakfast, on the table in readiness for her aunt's return. She sat by her uncle's bed, playing a lively tune on the zither to enliven the poor invalid and to make him, if possible, forget his pains. As Elsa entered with the stranger, the latter paused at the open door and viewed with pleasure the lovely picture of the zither player. Susan kept on undisturbed until she had finished; for she took it for granted that everyone loved music.

"Is that your daughter?" asked the stranger, as the sounds of the last chords died away.

"No, sir," answered Elsa, "she is my husband's niece from Bohemia, and she has been here a short while."

The herb gatherer approached the sick man, examined his stiffened limbs and spoke consolingly to him. He took from his box some green, strong-smelling herbs. He directed Elsa to boil them and to bathe the affected parts with the liquid. The spry and willing Susan at once took the matter in hand and quickly put the herbs in a pot which she set over the fire. The mixture soon boiled, and the stranger himself washed the sufferer's limbs.

When payment was mentioned he declined any reimbursement, requesting only that he might rest with them for an hour or two. Quietly he observed the active movements of Susan who was not idle for a single moment. After she had attended to the arrangement of the little room, and had split and piled the wood, she asked her aunt what further was to be done.

"Can you spin, my child?" asked Mother Elsa.

Susan shook her head.

"Then I'll teach you," said Elsa. She took the spindle and showed the attentive damsel how with one hand she drew the thread and at the same time turned the spindle with the other.

The stranger looked on and said, "My good woman, let me be her instructor. I'll teach her much more quickly on an entirely new instrument which I myself have invented. I must leave now for a couple of hours to attend to some business in the next village, but I shall return in the afternoon and bring what I have promised." With friendly farewell he left the house.

The sun was about to set as the stranger once more entered the room. He brought an implement which up to that time was entirely unknown to the good people. It was a spinning wheel, finely made of beautiful white wood. The spindle, or distaff, was crowned with tender flax bound with a blue silk ribbon.

"Now, Susan, come here," said he to the astonished girl. "Give heed while I work." He turned the wheel swiftly. Elsa saw with surprise how much more quickly the work was done than with the old-fashioned spindle. The maiden quickly understood the workings of the new wheel and showed herself an apt scholar.

"The spinning wheel is yours," said the herb gatherer to Susan. "Spin industriously. Your work will bring a blessing. I shall send a merchant to you who will pay the highest price for your labor. You need then have no further anxiety about your daily bread."

He bade the good people farewell, declined all thanks, and soon disappeared in the neighboring wood.

Susan worked from morning till evening. Her

cheerful song accompanied the merry hum of the spinning wheel. The thread slipped rapidly through her skillful fingers, and uncle and aunt saw with amazement how beautifully and evenly and finely it was spun. A merchant who paid a high price for the work came every Saturday as the little family sat at breakfast.

Stephen, too, was much improved. His pains gradually disappeared; his stiff limbs became supple: and with his now partly healed hands he began to carve, for he longed ardently to make a spinning wheel for his dear Elsa. He was happy to be able to do something, and he worked hard to accomplish his task.

At last the wheel was finished and, in perfect order. Though it was neither so fine nor so ornamental as Susan's, it was just as useful. The wheels were like two sisters, one of whom is beautiful and the other plain, but both of whom perform their respective duties.

Other wheels soon followed Stephen's first effort, for all who saw the little brisk machine wished to own one. His hands had become stronger, and as a visible blessing rested on his work he accepted every order. He was so well paid that in a little while prosperity came to the humble dwelling. Mother Elsa and Susan spun with such industry that good returns rewarded their labor.

After the most pressing necessities in house furnishing and clothing had been procured, Elsa went one day to the nearest town to visit the annual fair. She wanted to buy a bed for the beloved adopted daughter. Up to the present time, Susan had slept on straw, and the good woman wished now to prepare a pleasant surprise for her. When she reached the town she hurried to the store of a merchant who, besides many other articles, sold beds. She soon found what suited her, but the price was much more than her store of ready money. She sadly emptied her little leather purse, counted the money over and over, but it was pointless. She was forced to postpone the purchase until later.

She was standing in the street, lost in thought, when she suddenly heard a voice saying, "God greet you, dame Elsa. I suppose you're buying house furnishings for handsome Susan."

She turned quickly and beheld the friendly countenance of her benefactor, the herb gatherer. Astonished, she held out both hands to him; her grateful heart overflowed in warm, thankful words. She told him that her husband was almost entirely recovered, and that the spinning wheel had brought a blessing to their home. After the stranger had listened with great interest and had charged her with greetings for Stephen and Susan, he took his leave, pressing at the same time something into her hand. The next moment he was lost in the crowd.

Elsa, as if in a dream, looked at her half-open hand. She found there the exact sum required to make her purchase. She soon completed her bargain, and beaming with joy departed for the nearest inn. There she met young farmer Michel of her own village. He offered to take her and her purchase home in his basket wagon.

She gladly accepted the friendly offer and soon reached her home in comfort.

As the young farmer brought dame Elsa to her door, the beautiful Susan sat at the open window, busily turning her wheel and singing a cheerful song in a sweet voice. Michel listened, and so great was his admiration that he forgot to help the worthy Elsa out of the wagon. Susan hurried to welcome her aunt, helped her tenderly to the ground, grasped the bed with strong arms and brought it inside. The farmer looked quietly on, and saw with pleasure the cheerful activity of the beautiful maiden.

He said to himself, "Ah! Michel, if you could only bring her with you to your lonesome home on the farm. She would certainly be a loving and industrious wife." He might have said this out loud had not Elsa come forward quickly to give him a hearty handshake and a thankful farewell. He glanced toward the window at which he had first seen Susan, but as she was no longer there, he turned the wagon and started for his home outside the straggling village.

Next Sunday, after the pastor had uttered the last words of the divine service, there was a timid knock at the door of Stephen's humble abode, and farmer Michel entered with friendly greeting. After he had admired Stephen's last work, a beautiful wheel, and had praised Susan's fine spinning, he told the family that he desired to marry, and that it was in their power to help him. In a few but sincere and heartfelt words, he proposed for Susan's hand.

The astonished girl couldn't believe that so respectable and well-to-do a farmer should woo her at

first. With hearty consent, the maiden clasped his offered hand. She made but one condition, that her dear adoptive parents should go with her to enjoy life, free from care, in her new home. The happy lover willingly agreed, as it was a new proof of the grateful and affectionate heart of his future wife. The wedding was to be held in four weeks. It would then be exactly one year since Susan, as a homeless wanderer, had sought and found not only a home, but love and affection with her relatives.

Joy reigned in the little home. The aged couple blessed the hour when the orphaned girl had come to them. All kinds of good fortune had come with her. The only thing that saddened the otherwise happy Susan was the fact that she must enter the comfortable home of her husband and bring absolutely nothing with her.

She had neither money nor dowry, not even a web of linen. Everything she had thus far earned had been cheerfully spent on her adoptive parents, for whom she so ardently desired a comfortable life

With her head resting in her hands, she sat one day at the window sighing over her poverty. Her long, blond tresses hung down her back. Her foot leaned lightly on the treadle of her spinning wheel and her eyes rested thoughtfully on the spindle. A shadow glided before her. Looking up she recognized the merchant, who nodded cordially to her.

"God greet you, young bride," he said, "I heard but yesterday the news of your approaching marriage. I wish you all kinds of good fortune and peace and joy. I have laid a little wedding gift on the table for you. You will not need to make your fingers sore with spinning to fill chest and wardrobe with linen for your new home. Look well at me with your dear blue eyes, for you see the old merchant today for the last time."

Susan would gladly have invited him to visit her in her future home, but he had disappeared and he was nowhere to be seen.

She rushed to inspect the wedding gift. On the table lay six webs of the very finest linen and on them a slip of paper on which was written, "A bridal gift for the industrious Susan." She called her adoptive parents, and half laughing, half crying showed them her rich bridal present.

The old couple shook their heads and whispered of magic. The name of Rübezahl was uttered. "For," said they, "an ordinary merchant could never afford such a gift." But they rejoiced heartily over the good fortune of their adopted child who, in the fullness of her joy, embraced them over and over.

It was a sunny day when the beautiful Susan left the village church on the arm of her happy bridegroom. Every eye rested with pleasure on her graceful figure. A wreath of myrtle crowned her golden locks. The white bosom cloth, modestly folded, lifted itself out of the black satin waist on which hung a gold medal, the gift of the bridegroom. A many-flounced skirt of blue cloth completed her costume.

When she was outside the churchyard wall, the herb collector advanced and handed her a magnificent bouquet, saying, "You bring your husband the very best dowry — piety, industry and meekness. As long as you possess these three virtues, these flowers shall never fade, and your fortune, like them, shall always bloom, fresh and fair."

After he had extended his hand to the pair, he left, and from the lips of all present rose the name of "Rübezahl." It was indeed Rübezahl who, in the form of the herb collector and of the merchant, had brought blessings and prosperity to the humble home.

(ORIGINAL) EPILOGUE

The story of Beautiful Susan, the last of this series, shows Rübezahl at his best. During his many travels through his upper domains, he was the hero of many such adventures. Among the honest, simple-hearted people of Silesia and Bohemia, the part he played as the linen merchant and herb gatherer is dwelt upon with much pleasure. Even at the present day the story is still well-known and often related; it is ever new.

We have spared our young readers the less favorable side of Rübezahl's character. In his anger, especially when called by his mock name, he is represented as pitiless. Woe betide the thoughtless fellow whose daring would lead him to insult the invisible but often present Mountain Lord.

His adventure with Emma. as related in the first story formed the basis of these daring insults. Many times he was addressed aloud as "Maiden Robber," "Turnip Counter," and "Cheated One."

It might be of interest to add that prince Ratibor, the affianced of princess Emma and later her husband, built the town of Ratibor on the river Oder. This town exists to the present day, giving another proof of the long life of the names of places. Frequently names remain after their very meaning has been forgotten in the lapse of ages. In fact the mountain range where Rübezahl's deeds were performed continues to be called the Riesengebirge or giant's mountains; a tribute to the power and extent of the sway of this mighty spirit.